The Urbana Free Library

To renew materials call
217-367-4057

	DATE DUE		
	DEC 0 8 2010	JUL 0 5 2011	

Queen of Secrets

JENNY MEYERHOFF

FARRAR STRAUS GIROUX
NEW YORK

9|10
#17⁰⁰

Distributed in Canada by D&M Publishers, Inc.
Printed in May 2010 in the United States of America
by RR Donnelley, Harrisonburg, Virginia
Designed by Jay Colvin
First edition, 2010
1   3   5   7   9   10   8   6   4   2

www.fsgteen.com

Library of Congress Cataloging-in-Publication Data
Meyerhoff, Jenny.
    Queen of secrets / Jenny Meyerhoff.— 1st ed.
        p.   cm.
    Summary: Fifteen-year-old Essie Green, an orphan who has been raised by her
secular Jewish grandparents in Michigan, experiences conflicting loyalties and
confusing emotions when her aunt, uncle, and cousin move back from New York,
and her very religious cousin tries to fit in with the other football players at Essie's
high school, one of whom is Essie's popular new boyfriend.
    ISBN: 978-0-374-32628-9
    [1. Identity—Fiction.   2. Secrets—Fiction.   3. Interpersonal relations—
Fiction.   4. Jews—Fiction.   5. Cousins—Fiction.   6. Grandparents—
Fiction.   7. Orphans—Fiction.   8. Conduct of life—Fiction.   9. High schools—
Fiction.   10. Schools—Fiction.]   I. Title.

PZ7.M571753Im 2010
[Fic]—dc22

                                                                2008055561

For Peter

The king loved Esther more than all the women,
and she won more of his grace and favor than all the
other girls; so that he set the royal crown upon
her head and made her queen.
—Esther 2:17

Then Mordechai said to Esther: "Do not imagine that
you will be able to escape in the King's palace any
more than the rest of the Jews."
—Esther 4:13

Queen of Secrets

1

I didn't know how I managed to make the varsity cheerleading squad. I only knew that if Austin King was ever going to notice me, I had to have one of those purple-and-gold uniforms. They gave the girls who wore them an aura of extra prettiness. Even the girls who didn't need the help, like Hayden Walsh. Tall, blond, perfect: *she* was the image that popped in my head whenever I thought of the word *cheerleader*. I, on the other hand, probably never popped into anyone's mind at all. At least, I hadn't last year, but this year, I hoped, would be different.

Monday morning, when Nana dropped me off for the first preseason cheerleading practice, Hayden and her best friend, Lara, walked right by our car.

"Hi, Essie," Hayden called. She was my cheerleading big sister, a senior, and one of Austin's good friends. I couldn't believe my luck when Ms. Young paired us together at cheerleading camp last month, but I jumped when she called my name. I hadn't really expected Hayden to do anything more than help me learn new cheers, and maybe decorate my locker on my birthday.

"Hi!" I called back, my voice shaking. I said goodbye to Nana and jogged to catch up with them.

"How was the rest of your summer?" Hayden asked me, opening the school door.

"Fantastic!" I said, even though I'd spent most of it helping Nana garden, dancing alone in my bedroom, and daydreaming about Austin. Sara, my best friend, had spent most of her vacation working at Faber's Art Supply, and Zoe and Skye, our other two friends, had both gone away for the summer. I was more than ready for school to start next week. "How was your summer?" I asked.

"Amazing," Hayden said as she went inside. Then she stopped short. "I need to tell you guys something." She glanced at Lara. "Remember those soccer players who crashed my party on Saturday? I hooked up with one of them last night."

Lara shoved Hayden playfully on the shoulder. "No way. Who?"

"John Barstow," Hayden whispered, taking a deep breath. "It got intense."

The thrill of Hayden confiding in me tingled, but I had no idea what to say. I hadn't been at her party. Or even been invited. And I'd never kissed anyone. My friends weren't really the kinds of girls who hooked up. I wasn't sure I even knew exactly what Hayden meant. Kissing, or something more? "Congratulations!" I spluttered.

Hayden stopped walking and looked at me funny. Not congratulations? "Uh, who's John Barstow?" I asked.

"He's a *junior*," said Lara, wrinkling her nose as if she smelled something rotten.

"He's hot," said Hayden. "He's an amazing kisser, and, unlike most guys at this school, he's taller than me."

"He's still a junior," Lara answered.

When we got to the gym, most of the other cheerleaders were already there. Hayden tossed her gym bag into the corner. I put mine next to hers and followed her and Lara to the equipment closet. I held my breath as we helped carry out the mats. They smelled like my grandfather's feet.

"You aren't thinking of making this into something more than a hookup, are you?" asked Lara. "Because that would look really desperate."

"Everyone start stretching!" Hayden shouted to the room without answering Lara. Ms. Young, our coach, still hadn't arrived. As the captain, Hayden ran practice when Ms. Young wasn't around. She sat between Lara and me and reached forward to touch her toes. "I don't care how it looks. I'm having fun. Worry about your own love life."

Lara straddled her legs and stretched sideways without answering.

"You can pretend you don't know what I'm talking about." Hayden winked at me, then turned back to Lara. "But I saw the way you were looking at Austin on Saturday night."

Lara ignored Hayden again and touched her toes. I froze in the middle of my stretch. Lara liked Austin?

Hayden teased, "What do you think, Essie? Wouldn't they make a cute couple?"

Ms. Young ran into the gym and saved me from having to answer.

"Sorry I'm late, everyone! When you've finished stretching, I want five laps and then twenty each of crunches, lower abs, push-ups, and squats."

Ms. Young went into the equipment closet to get her clipboard, and Lara and Hayden stood up to start the laps.

"You coming?" Hayden asked me.

I shook my head. "I still need to stretch my calves," I said. I didn't want to hear any more about Lara and Austin.

Hayden ran off, and I tried to calm my heart. It beat like I'd just run a marathon.

I watched the other girls jogging. Lara glanced at Ms. Young to make sure she wasn't looking, then imitated the cheerleader in front of her running with splayed legs. She and Hayden cracked up.

Last year, I used to watch Austin and his friends from a million miles away, a lowly freshman with a huge crush. This year, I'd convinced myself that things could be different. I'd finally grown some curves. (A lot of curves, actually.) I'd made the cheerleading squad. There was an outside shot that Austin might notice me. But Lara was a senior. She was tall and willowy, with shiny brown hair that swung in a perfect bob. Even more important than that, she had experience. She knew how to talk to guys, to flirt with them, to make them like her. If she liked Austin, then cheerleading uniform or not, I'd never be more than a sophomore nobody.

AFTER CHEERLEADING, some of the seniors decided to watch the end of football practice. Hayden called to me from the gym doorway as I was packing up my bag.

"Baby sis!"

I looked up at her. Her smile was genuine.

"Come hang with us." She motioned me over with her head.

My thoughts raced. Us? *Us* could mean Austin. I shoved my gym shoes in my bag, slid on my flip-flops, and ran to catch up with them.

As we headed over toward the field, a bunch of football players turned to check us out. But when we sat down on the squishy rubber surface of the track, just to the left of the players' bench, my stomach twisted. They probably weren't checking *us* out, I realized. *I* couldn't be included in that group. The other girls wore sexy workout clothes. Sports bras and shorts with the tops folded over, their limbs perfectly tanned. Their hair hung long, smooth, and neat.

Secretly I'd been believing that once I was a cheerleader I'd suddenly turn into someone else, a Cheerleader with a capital C. A girl with sleek hair, a perfect body, and a perfect life. But here I was, in my baggy T-shirt and gray sweat shorts, still me. My grandmother wouldn't buy me tight clothes. I grabbed the edge of my shirt and tied it in a knot. Then I felt my ponytail and tried to smooth back the frizz. I couldn't just slip the rubber band off and brush my fingers through my hair like they had. Curly hair didn't work that way.

Suddenly I felt small and out of place. If Austin ever looked over at us, I would stand out in the worst way. Four gorgeous girls in a row, and then me.

I searched the field for him and saw him settle in behind center, quarterbacking for the gold team in a scrimmage. He took the snap and dropped back for a pass. The left tackle and left guard both missed their blocks. The defensive end came in from Austin's blind side and drove his helmet into Austin's back. I drew a sharp breath in, then looked at Hayden next to me, hoping she hadn't noticed. She was leaning back with her face turned to the sun and her eyes closed.

Coach Ryan was all over the guy, yelling at him for hitting the QB during practice. Austin hobbled over to the bench, wincing and trying not to show it. I could have stared at him all day, but then I heard Coach Ryan yell, "Gruenberg!" My eyes jerked away. What was *he* doing here?

"Let's see what you can do." Coach motioned him onto the field.

Gruenberg was Micah Gruenberg, my first cousin. I barely knew him. His family had just moved back to Pershing, Michigan, from New York a week ago. I hadn't even known he was on the football team until now. He ran over from the side where he'd been taking practice kicks. He was going to make a field goal attempt for the gold team. Coach wanted him to try a long one— maybe forty yards. I scooted forward to watch.

"I hope he's decent," said Hayden, sitting back up and nodding her head toward Micah.

"I know him," I said. "He's—"

Lara cut me off. "Compared to Keith, anyone would be decent," she said in a low voice. "But I heard he's weird."

I bit my words back into my mouth. Where had she heard that? Austin?

"Weird how?" asked the girl to Lara's left.

8

Lara shrugged.

Hayden leaned over to me. "See number 27?" She pointed to one of the players, and I nodded, but I was still thinking about *weird*.

"He was our kicker last year," she said. "He sucked."

Micah stood behind the holder and rubbed his hands together. The cheerleaders on the other side of Lara started talking about the best way to do smoky eyes and Lara and Hayden turned around to join the conversation. I had nothing to add. I knew zero about makeup; Nana still wouldn't let me wear it. I kept watching the field and eavesdropping on the players near the end of the bench.

Number 33 said, "No way he makes that."

On the field, Micah rocked his body back and forth. His lips moved silently, almost like he was praying. What if he *was* praying? His family was very religious.

The center snapped the ball and Micah took three steps forward and let his kick loose. He kept mumbling until the ball soared cleanly between the goal posts, then he let out a deep exhale and jogged toward the sidelines.

"Sweet," said number 27, patting Micah on the back.

I was about to tap Hayden on the shoulder to brag about my better-than-decent-new-kicker cousin when I heard Harrison, Austin's best friend, shout, "Hey, Rabbi! Nice kick!"

A flicker of irritation twitched across Micah's face, but he shook it away and said, "Thanks."

Harrison turned to the player next to him. "What? What'd I say?" He called to Micah. "Hey, it was a compliment."

Micah nodded and went to sit on the bench.

When football practice ended, Harrison came over and sat down in front of Hayden and Lara. He motioned for Austin to join us, but Austin was busy cleaning the dirt and grass out of his cleats. He made eye contact with Harrison and shook his head ever so slightly. His damp shaggy blond hair fell over his forehead in clumps as he went back to work on his shoes.

"King," Harrison called this time. Austin looked up slowly, and Harrison motioned him over again. Finally Austin rolled his eyes and tossed his cleats on the ground. Then he joined us and sat down facing me.

It was the closest I'd ever been to him, our knees practically touching. His eyes were two different shades of brown, darker in the center, then lighter at the edges. I inhaled deeply and caught the scent of the sweat on his forehead. Little sparks of electricity hovered around my body. I smoothed my hair back as much as I could.

"What are you guys doing later?" Harrison asked Hayden.

"Going to the club, maybe." She stretched her arms out, admiring them. "Work on my tan."

He leaned forward. "I'll work on your tan."

"You wish." Hayden laughed and pushed him back. He bumped into Austin, and Austin's knee knocked against mine. The polyester of his football pants scratched against my skin.

"What are you guys going to do?" Lara asked, turning to Austin.

Harrison looked at Austin, too. "What do you want to do? Go swimming?"

Austin shrugged. "I'm not in the mood to swim. You guys should go without me."

For a split second, I thought I saw Lara give Austin a dirty look. Then she put her hand around Harrison's bicep. The bottom of his sleeve hugged the top curve of his muscle. "I think you got bigger this summer," she said.

He puffed his chest. "Two hundred push-ups a day."

I looked at Austin's biceps. They weren't as big as Harrison's, but I liked them better. I wondered what he'd do if I put my hand around his arm. Probably think I was crazy.

"*Two hundred?* Yeah, right." A junior named Eric, almost as big as Harrison, stood a couple of feet away from us. Another junior, Wyatt, stood behind him, like a shadow.

"Are you calling me a liar?" Harrison stared hard at Eric. "You wanna see?"

Austin's shoulders drooped, like he was tired, and he sighed. "Don't," he said to Harrison. "He's not worth it."

Eric glared at Austin, but Austin didn't seem to notice. His eyes were on Harrison. So were Wyatt's, but his expression wasn't concern. It was more like awe.

"Harrison, what happened when you visited MSU last week?" he asked. "Doesn't your dad know the coach? He played there, right?"

"They offered me preferred walk-on." From Harrison's tone, I guessed that wasn't so great. Austin tilted his head and watched Harrison carefully.

"Isn't that a glorified no?" Eric asked.

Harrison's jaw twitched.

"Best-case scenario, you'd be on the practice team," Eric said. "Anyway, their roster's probably been full since June. Everything happens *junior* year."

"Not everything, loser. There are still plenty of schools looking for players," Harrison said, but his voice didn't sound convinced.

"If you want to play Division Two," said Eric.

Harrison turned to Austin, his face a snarl. "I don't think these guys understand the respect they owe seniors."

Austin stood up. The barest wave of annoyance washed across his face before he set his jaw and stepped close enough to Eric that they were eye to eye. "You think you can do better? You'll be lucky if you get to play *this* year. Especially if you keep missing blocks like today. My ribs thank you."

"That wasn't his fault," Wyatt began, but when Austin glared at him, Wyatt lowered his eyes and kept his mouth shut.

Eric shrugged. "You weren't supposed to be live during that drill."

"You still should have protected me." Austin glanced over at the messy players' bench. "Clean up the water bottles and bring all the towels back to the locker room."

Eric narrowed his eyes at Austin. "Are you serious?"

Austin folded his arms. "You need to respect the seniors."

"Let's just do it," said Wyatt. He started picking up the bottles while Eric watched.

Austin sat back down a little farther from me. I shifted positions so that if he moved our knees would bump again, but he was lost in thought. Then Micah walked over and squatted next to me.

"Hi, Essie," he said.

"Hi," I answered. Everyone shifted to watch us. The word *weird* pulsed in my thoughts.

Lara squinted at me, then at Micah. One of her eyebrows arched up, and a half-smile crept onto her lips. She was looking at the thing on Micah's head, the little hat. He called it a kippah, and it was a Jewish head-covering. He wore it all the time. I thought it was really strange the first time I saw it, too. Maybe that kind of thing didn't stand out much in New York, but I'd never seen anyone wear one in Pershing. Especially not at football practice. The Jewish people in my town probably wore them at synagogue, but I wouldn't know. I never went.

"Beanie," Austin said, raising his hand to Micah for a high five. "You rocked it."

Micah hesitated for a second, then slapped Austin's hand. "Thanks." He turned back to me. "How's it going?"

"Good," I said. "Your kick was great. I thought most high school kickers used a two-step approach and a straight-on kick."

Micah started to answer, but Austin let out a snort of laughter. I looked over at him, my cheeks on fire. I'd been reading everything I could about football and watching instructional videos on the Internet so that I wouldn't say something stupid if I ever got to talk to him. That obviously hadn't worked.

I turned back to Micah, "Do I have it backward?"

He shook his head. "No, you're right. I'm just more used to kicking soccer-style because I played soccer at my old school. It's more accurate, too."

"Sorry," Austin said. He'd stopped laughing, but his eyes still twinkled. "You caught me off guard." He angled his head toward

Hayden and Lara. "These two usually comment on who looks hot, not on playing technique."

"You should have tried out for football instead of cheerleading," Lara said to me. Then to Austin she added, "Maybe she secretly wants to be a guy."

"Or tackle one." Austin waggled his eyebrows.

I looked down at my feet. I'd have to remember to keep my football thoughts to myself. When I looked back up, Austin was smiling. I tried to smile back, but panic seeped through my body. Why was he still looking at me?

"What's your name again?" Austin asked.

My stomach dropped into my lap.

"Uh, my name?" I wanted to close my eyes and disappear. Was I seriously blanking on my name?

"Essie," I finally said, pinching the front of my shirt and fanning it in and out. My body temperature had risen a thousand degrees. "Essie Green."

"Nice to meet you, Essie Green." Austin stood up. "See you guys later," he said. "I'm going to hit the showers."

Harrison followed him, but Micah stayed behind, and Lara stared him down like he had a third eyeball.

"I guess I should shower, too," he said. "I'll see you later, Essie."

Lara tilted her head, shielded her eyes from the sun, and studied me. Her look gave me goose bumps. "What's up between you and Beanie Boy?" she asked when Micah was out of earshot.

I opened my mouth to tell her that Micah was my cousin, but

no sound came out. I could just hear Lara calling me Beanie Girl, or even worse, when she knew.

"Do you *like* him?" Lara asked.

"No!" I said, louder than I'd meant to.

"I have a feeling Essie likes someone else," said Hayden, bumping shoulders with me.

I shook my head. Was it that obvious?

"Looks like you've got some competition," she said to Lara.

Lara smiled at me in a way that wasn't a smile at all, then she turned to Hayden and narrowed her eyes. "I don't know what you're talking about."

"Me neither," I said with a laugh as fake as I felt. If Austin had to choose between Lara and Beanie Boy's cousin, was there really any choice at all?

2

The problem with my uncle's family moving back to Pershing was that I was supposed to feel some deep connection to them because we were blood-related, but the truth was I didn't feel anything. I hardly knew them anymore. When I was really little, maybe five years old, I used to wish sometimes that I was part of their family. That was two years after my parents' death, and my uncle's family had already moved away by then, but I still remembered them. A little.

Whenever Nana was having one of her bad days, crying and staying in bed all day, I'd pretend that my aunt Shelli was on an airplane flying to Michigan to get me. She'd whisk me off to New York, where she'd be my new mother and Micah would be my brother, and I'd never have to play Candy Land alone again. But after the months and years went by without visits, my uncle's family became fuzzier and fuzzier in my memory. They started to seem less and less real—more like characters in a book than flesh-and-blood people.

At first, after my uncle's family moved to New York, I wondered why we never saw them anymore, why we couldn't visit. I worried, probably like all little kids would, that it was because of me. Nana's excuse was that visiting was too expensive, so one day, when I was in first grade, I took all my stuffed animals to school and sold every one to my classmates for a quarter apiece. I came home that day with a bag full of change, so excited to tell Nana that we could finally visit. The pride I'd been feeling shriveled as Nana's face crumpled. "No, sugar," she said, her voice catching. "Papa and Uncle Steve aren't ready."

Her words made no sense to me, but I didn't ask her to explain. Nana already spent too much time crying and staying in bed. Suddenly I understood that my uncle's family was part of the reason we couldn't go to New York. It was their fault, and I didn't want to visit them anymore. We hardly ever spoke of them after that.

Over the years, however, bits of information slipped out, so I knew that a year after my parents died, something happened between Papa and Uncle Steve. A rift so big my uncle moved his family away and didn't speak to his own father for five years, until Papa was diagnosed with prostate cancer. He was fine now. Nobody ever *really* doubted he'd survive, but it was enough for Nana and Aunt Shelli to finally convince Papa and Uncle Steve to try to put their relationship back together.

For the past several years, Nana, Papa, and I had spent awkward Thanksgivings in New York, and now Uncle Steve was back in Michigan to take over Papa's accounting business. We were going to try to be a family again.

Since we now lived in the same town, reconciliation had moved into high gear. Case in point: it was Friday night, and what was

I going to do? Hang out with my best friend, Sara? Watch reality TV? No. I was on my way to a Shabbat dinner at my uncle's house. I'd never been to a Shabbat dinner in my entire life.

I sat pinned to the backseat of the car because there was something wrong with my seat belt. It wouldn't give. I unbuckled, let the belt fully retract, then tried again. It didn't help. I dropped my head backward against the headrest. "Are we going to have to pray tonight?" I whined.

I didn't see why we had to go to a Shabbat dinner. Why not a regular dinner on a Sunday night? When we'd gone to New York for Thanksgiving, Nana and Papa had always taken me to a play on Friday nights. Everyone seemed fine with that arrangement.

"We are going to be good guests and participate in any way your aunt and uncle would like," Nana said. She squeezed Papa's shoulder. "Right?"

Papa humphed, but nodded. He didn't believe in religion. When I was ten, the night before Papa had surgery for his prostate cancer, Uncle Steve had come to visit. It was the first time my grandfather and uncle had seen each other in years, and they could barely speak or look at one another. We all sat together in the dining room drinking tea and not talking until finally Uncle Steve asked, "Would you like to pray?"

Papa shook his head. "Praying is wishful thinking—false comfort for people afraid of life. And death. I've seen enough of both," he said. "I'm not afraid."

A tiny needle of fear pricked my heart. I didn't want Papa not to fear death.

Uncle Steve blew on his tea. "I'm going to pray for you any- way," he said.

Papa shrugged, and I felt guilty for being relieved. I'd never had to go to religious school or religious services or religious any- thing, and that was fine by me, but maybe in certain circumstances it was nice to know someone who prayed.

WHEN WE GOT to my uncle's house, Nana shooed Micah and me away for some quality cousin-bonding time.

"You kids go play," Nana said. "We'll call you when dinner's ready."

Micah turned to me with confusion in his green eyes as all the adults walked away from us into the kitchen.

"Sorry," I said, "but you're going to have to get used to it. Nana still thinks we're ten years old."

"Got it," said Micah. "In that case, do you want to play Battle- ship?"

I laughed. "Why not?"

I was long past wishing Micah was my brother, but I didn't know how I felt about him moving back to my town. Part of me was excited to get to know him, to finally experience having a cousin, but another part of me just wasn't interested. I'd gone the past eleven years without having any real relationship with Micah, and my life was just fine. I didn't want some person I barely knew to mess it up. Because the deep-down truth was, a part of me agreed with Lara. He did seem kind of weird.

We went up to Micah's bedroom, and I sat down on the bed while he got the game from the top shelf in his closet. In the corner of the room was a keyboard with boxes piled around it and an already overfull bookshelf. On the walls were a New York Giants poster and a picture of Albert Einstein riding a bicycle.

"I didn't realize you were on the football team," I said as Micah settled across from me and handed me my game board.

"I wasn't," he said. "Not until today. I spent the whole week practicing with the team on a trial basis. But Coach Ryan finally made it official."

"That's great!" I said. "You must be excited."

Micah opened up his game board and began deliberately placing his ships without answering right away. "Yeah. Sort of."

I positioned my ships randomly around the grid, wondering if Micah's lack of enthusiasm had anything to do with Lara's comment. Did I know him well enough to suggest that he might want to stop wearing his beanie to school? In New York he'd gone to a Jewish day school. That was probably another universe compared to public school.

"B-5," Micah said, starting the game.

"Miss," I answered. "Only *sort of* excited? It's a huge commitment. Are you sure you want to be on the team if you only feel 'sort of' about it?"

Micah fingered the little white pegs used to mark misses while he thought about my question. Then he nodded his head emphatically. "I am excited. I just need a mental readjustment."

"A mental readjustment?" I echoed.

"Well, I'd been hoping to get some action," he explained. "I wanted to be a wide receiver, but it looks like I'll just be a backup receiver. Practices only. My real position is kicker."

"That's an important position," I said, tracing my finger over the Battleship grid. "Lots of glory potential. E-10."

"Hit," he said, surprised. I guessed he didn't remember that we'd played many games of Battleship the first year I'd ever visited him. His strategy was always to place his ships at the edges of the board. Some things hadn't changed. I stuck the red peg into my board and Micah said, "I know you're right. I'm sure I'll feel different when I get to know the guys."

"Yeah. Probably," I answered, my uncertainty written all over my voice.

"What?" he asked.

I bit my lower lip. If I told him the truth, I could wind up being the bad guy. Then again, if there was something simple he could do, he might want to know. *I'd* want to know. "Do you think . . . " I started, then stopped. Suddenly I felt embarrassed, as if I was about to say something impossibly rude.

"What?" he asked again.

"I don't know," I said. "I was just going to say . . . your, uh . . . " I put my hand on the crown of my head. Just saying the word out loud, *kippah*, felt strange to me. Nana and Papa didn't even call it that. They used a different word, *yarmulke*, which was worse, in my opinion.

"Oh," he said, a hand rising to his head. "Oh. Are you serious?" Micah laughed but it was the kind of laugh that sounded like disbelief. "I know the guys joke about it, but . . . do we go to some kind of neo-Nazi school?"

"No!" I shook my head firmly. "Definitely no. It's just that I've never seen anyone wear one of those to school before." I pointed at his head. "No one at Pershing has. It's like you're wearing a cape or a tool belt or something. It just doesn't make sense and it looks kind of . . . weird." My cheeks grew warm. Had I really just told my cousin that I thought he looked weird?

"Well, I'm wearing it for a reason," Micah said. "It wouldn't be weird to wear a tool belt during shop class."

"Oh, I know," I said, feeling my blush grow deeper. "I'm just saying people probably aren't used to it. They might think you should just wear those things at synagogue."

Micah shrugged like it was no big deal, but the annoyance that passed over his face gave him away. "Well, they'll have to get used to it," he said, exhaling loudly. "I can't change who I am."

"Right," I agreed, nodding my head, but not feeling so sure. I couldn't imagine Lara ever not thinking it was weird.

"J-3," he said, as if the conversation was over, forgotten, Battleship the only thing left on his mind. But his lips were drawn in a thin line.

"Miss."

I wondered if *I* could stop thinking it was weird.

FIFTEEN MINUTES LATER my aunt called us downstairs, but before we sat to eat, she wanted us to light the Shabbat candles. "Esther, would you say the blessing?" she asked when we walked into the kitchen.

Hardly. I looked over my shoulder, joking, like there was another Esther in the room who knew what my aunt was talking about. "I don't think I know that one," I said, then reminded her, "And everyone calls me Essie now."

Aunt Shelli nodded. "Essie," she said. "I'll teach you."

She didn't ask if I wanted to learn.

We gathered around the windowsill, except Papa, who went to the bathroom. Aunt Shelli gave me a lacy pink kippah that looked like a doily. She wore one, too. I could just imagine what the cheerleaders and football players would say if they saw us.

Aunt Shelli lit the candles and made me circle my hands over the flames to gather the light to my face. I covered my eyes and repeated some Hebrew words after her. I had no idea what I was saying; it felt ridiculous. The doily kept slipping off, and I peeked twice to see if everyone else was covering their eyes, too. They were. I was surprised to see that Nana knew the words.

When we finished the blessing, the glow from the candles made the room soft and peaceful. I felt guilty for having peeked, but the next time they tried to get me to do Jewish stuff, I was going to hide in the bathroom like Papa. All this religion felt like superstition to me.

"Okay," said Aunt Shelli, pointing toward the dining room. "Time for dinner."

Uncle Steve said, "I guess someone should find Dad and tell him the coast is clear."

WE SAT DOWN at the table, set with a mix of formal and disposable: fancy crystal and paper napkins. A salad, still in the supermarket container, sat next to a china platter with a huge braided bread on it that my aunt said was called challah. Its scent was warm and yeasty. Aunt Shelli filled everyone's wineglass, including mine, and Uncle Steve handed Papa a kippah. Papa held the black fabric between two fingers and I thought he was going to drop it on the table, but he put it on his head. It wouldn't lie flat. Then Uncle Steve began to sing a long prayer over the wine and the bread. At times, Micah and my aunt sang with him. I guiltily checked my watch and wondered how long before this whole Shabbat dinner would be over. I didn't mind getting to know my family, really I didn't, but I could think of a thousand things I'd rather be doing besides praying. For example, fantasizing about Austin King. Or Googling him. Or riding my bike by his house.

What if I'd gotten my wish when I was little? Would I have done this every weekend?

When the prayer was finished, Aunt Shelli began to serve the meal. She brought the chicken out in an aluminum baking pan and placed it on heavy-duty paper plates. "Sorry about the dishes. We still haven't finished unpacking," she said, pointing to a pile of boxes in the living room.

"We're not fancy," said Nana, taking a bite of salad. "But I wish you had let us host."

At the same exact time my aunt said, "We wanted to entertain in our new place," and my uncle said, "Your house isn't kosher."

The two answers hung in the air. Papa rolled his eyes, and Nana shot him a warning look. Aunt Shelli put her hand on my uncle's shoulder, but her eyes darted to me and were filled with sadness. Somehow that one tiny sentence set everyone on edge. I looked at Micah—maybe he knew what the big deal was—but he was looking at me with pity in his eyes. Suddenly I realized *everyone* was looking at me.

Even though I couldn't think of any reason why, it seemed up to me to break the tension.

"Nana. Papa," I said. "Did you know that Micah made the football team?"

"Congratulations!" said Papa, a relieved smile spreading over his face.

Nana turned to Aunt Shelli. "We should work out a carpool for games. Essie's going to be a cheerleader."

"Nana!" I tried to catch Micah's eye. "Micah's sixteen. He can drive himself. And I can find my own ride."

It would have been bad enough if she'd asked *him* to give me a ride, but carpooling with Aunt Shelli? Complete humiliation. When would Nana realize I was growing up? I'd be able to drive *myself* in a few months. Then again, at least this was a normal kind of tension. Not the crazy stuff from a few minutes ago.

Aunt Shelli shook her head. "Unfortunately, we won't be able to make any of Micah's games." She looked at Uncle Steve, but he wouldn't meet her eyes. He took a bite of a drumstick and chewed angrily. "We'll drop Micah off before they start, and he'll walk home."

"That's silly," Papa said. "We'll drive him home."

Micah's cheeks went bright red. Walking probably seemed better than having your grandfather drive you. Or maybe he was planning to get a ride with one of the guys on the team. Maybe with Austin.

"That's okay, Papa." Micah unfolded his napkin and laid it on his lap. "All the games are on Friday nights."

Papa snorted, and Micah's eyes darted over to my uncle. Suddenly my brain clicked and I understood all the fuss. Friday nights were Shabbat dinners. Micah would have to miss them to be on the team. Even though my uncle was a Conservative Jew, not an Orthodox one, he was *very* observant. He didn't drive on Shabbat unless he was going to synagogue. I guessed he didn't want Micah to drive on Shabbat, either. Especially not for football.

The tension I'd hoped to ease was back and bigger than ever.

"Soccer games are on Sundays," my uncle said.

"I don't want to play soccer. I want to play football," Micah answered. "Besides, I can decide for myself how observant I want to be."

"It's just football, Steve," Papa said.

"Are you going to question how I raise my own son now?"

Nana shot Papa a look that clearly meant he shouldn't say anything else. My uncle sighed. I dug into my mashed potatoes and said a thousand thank-yous in my mind for the fact that I didn't have to worry about being Jewish. I mean, it wasn't too long ago that Micah was disagreeing with me when I suggested he take off his beanie and act *less* Jewish, and now he was arguing with his father, who wanted him not to drive and to act *more* Jewish. It was the kind of drama that could make your head explode.

AFTER DINNER we all went in the backyard to have dessert under the stars on Aunt Shelli and Uncle Steve's new teak furniture.

"I've never had backyard furniture before!" Aunt Shelli said, rubbing her arm along the chaise. "We didn't even have a back-yard in New York."

"It's beautiful," said Nana. "Make sure you cover it in the winter."

The night was warm, but someone in the neighborhood had lit a campfire. It made the air smell like fall even though it was just the end of August.

"We're looking forward to your recitals this year, Essie. It's been a long time since I've seen you dance." Aunt Shelli blew on her coffee, and the steam rose up into the night. "You used to wear a leotard and tutu every day when you were little."

Nana and Papa laughed, but I looked up, surprised. I didn't have any memories of Aunt Shelli watching me dance.

"I remember one of your recitals," Micah said. "At the end, after everyone left the stage, you just stood there. You didn't know what to do."

"I can't believe you remember that," said Aunt Shelli, laughing and looking at me like I was still that same adorable girl. "You've probably got it down pat now."

"Actually, I quit dance," I told her, "for cheerleading."

"Really? No more tap? Nancy, have you lost your Shirley Temple?" Aunt Shelli looked at Nana, who closed her eyes and inhaled deeply. Nana hadn't talked to me for a whole day after I quit. She took it personally.

"Shirley Temple was a little kid," I said.

"Well, I've offered to teach an Israeli dance class at the synagogue. I thought it would be a good way to reconnect with everyone," my aunt said. "You're more than welcome to come whenever you feel like moving your feet. I'd love your company."

Israeli dance? "Uh . . . I'll have to see how busy I am with cheerleading."

Aunt Shelli nodded, and the conversation moved on to boring accounting-business talk. Throughout the rest of the night, my aunt stole glances at me over and over again. Her looks were soft and full of love, and they made me want to scoot farther and farther into the corner of my chair, away from her. She barely knew me. How could she feel that way about me? She didn't even know that I'd started going by Essie, or that I'd quit dancing. And not that I wanted her for a mother anymore, but if she'd wanted that kind of relationship with me, I guessed she'd sort of missed her chance.

3

It was the first day of my sophomore year, and I had a stomach-ache. Not because I didn't want to go back. I wouldn't admit it to anyone, but I was happy to start school this year. I mean, I was a cheerleader and Austin actually knew I was alive. He knew my *name*. The stomachache was more about excitement, knowing that anything could happen, but having no idea what it would be.

Sara's yellow Volkswagen rolled into my driveway early, just like I'd asked her to, but when we got to Pershing the parking lot was already full. We had to park so far away we were practically in Antarctica. Austin's car, a black Jeep, sat in its usual spot by the entrance to the athletic fields. Sometimes he hung out there with his friends before school, but he wasn't there today. When we got to the front courtyard, I checked the benches and the groups of seniors hanging out on the grassy area by the school sign. He wasn't anywhere.

"Can you spend one second not looking for him?" Sara asked, sitting herself down next to an oak tree ringed by wood chips. "I can't take another year of watching you pine away."

She shook her head at me and pulled a sketch pad out of her backpack. Sara wrote a comic strip for the school paper, and for as long as I'd known her she was always drawing cartoons and comics. One of my earliest memories was of Sara giving me a comic strip at my parents' funeral. In the first panel a blond girl (her) was giving a curly-haired girl (me) a rainbow heart. In the second panel, we were both floating inside the heart.

"He's not worth it," Sara added, bopping me on the forehead with her pencil.

I tried not to feel annoyed and to remind myself that I could like whoever I wanted. Just because the whole school thought Austin was a player, and had spent half of last year talking about how he dumped Vi Davison because she wouldn't sleep with him, didn't mean *I* had to believe those rumors. Besides, I hadn't told Sara about my encounter with Austin at practice. She didn't know my status had risen.

"This year might be different," I said.

Sara eyed me as she leaned back against the tree and started drawing. "Spill, please. Did something happen?"

I thought about Austin asking me my name, and the way our knees brushed. "Words were exchanged," I said. "There was physical contact."

"Really?" Sara tapped her pencil against the edge of her paper. "Consensual?"

Leave it to Sara to poke a hole in the most exciting moment of my high school life so far. Sometimes I wondered if she cared more about making her point than she did about my feelings.

Either way, I didn't want to talk about Austin anymore. I pulled a magazine out of my backpack and started reading while she drew.

"*Seventeen?*" Sara rolled her eyes. "How can you read that? It totally perpetuates the beauty myth."

I looked up at her. Sara always thought she knew what was best for me. I guessed it came from being a year older.

"You know, I can make you look exactly like those girls," she said.

"What?" Since when did Sara know about clothes and makeup?

"I'm taking digital media this semester. Just give me your picture and I'll Photoshop you until you look as fake as they do."

"Ha ha." I should have known Sara was making fun. "There's lots of good information in these. Look, here's an article about going to college."

Sara grabbed the magazine from me.

"It's about gaining the freshman fifteen!" She laughed.

"It's just a little helpful advice," I said. I shoved the magazine back into my backpack and pointed over her shoulder. "There are Zoe and Skye."

"Where?" Sara scanned the crowd, then shouted their names, and they joined us.

"How was the trip?" Sara asked Skye.

"Amazing," Skye answered in her quiet voice. She and Sara were friends from newspaper, but Skye preferred creative writing. Over the summer she'd gone on a cross-country bus trip for teen writers. "I'm halfway through my novel." She touched the side of

Sara's head. "I love your hair like this." For the first day of school, Sara had done her hair in a bunch of twisted mini-buns, each with a different color band.

Sara shrieked. "You got a tattoo!" A tiny cloud was inked under Skye's right eye, toward the cheekbone.

"It looks good," I said. It accentuated her excellent bone structure. "How was theater camp?" I asked Zoe. A self-proclaimed theater geek, she was wearing a tiara and a vintage prom dress to start the school year off in style. And she answered me in song. At the top of her lungs. "I could have danced all night."

The group of guys at the next tree over stopped talking to look at us. They were not staring in a good way.

Last year I wore something Danskin or sweatpants with the word *dancer* on the butt nearly every day, because that was my role. We were the artist, the writer, the actress, and the dancer. Today I wore normal clothes. Tank top and shorts.

"Are we meeting at the benches after school?" Sara asked.

I shook my head. "I've got cheerleading practice."

"Oh yeah," she said. "That's going to take some getting used to."

"You're actually doing this?" Zoe asked.

"I thought Sara was joking," Skye added.

"Why do I have the feeling you guys won't be coming to my games?"

"We'll come," Sara said.

"Of course we'll come," Skye said. "We're your best friends."

"Thanks," I answered.

I checked the time on my phone. The first bell was going to

ring any second, and I still had to stop in at the office to pick up my driver's ed forms. I'd been fifteen for months already, and the first class was this Saturday. I didn't know why I was procrastinating. I hoped they had spaces left.

"I have to go," I said. "See you at lunch."

I headed toward school but stopped just outside the doors. Nerves wriggled around inside me so wildly I couldn't go inside. What if my stomachache was for nothing? What if *nothing* at all happened to me this year? I wanted something to happen. Something big. Something life-changing.

Please let it happen.

Then I saw a reflection in the glass door. Austin was walking up behind me. My brain turned to mush. When Austin got to the door, he pulled it open for me. A blast of air-conditioning escaped from the lobby and hit me in the face. Austin smiled at me like he had at practice, then his eyes traveled from my head down to my toes and back up. Sara would say there was something degrading about the way he looked at me, but it made my skin tingle. Like I was being seen for the first time.

He motioned for me to go inside. I didn't move at first. I didn't want him to stop looking, and I didn't have full control of my motor functions, either. So I stood there a second more, gawking at him like I'd done all freshman year.

"Essie, right?" he asked.

I nodded, and my shoulder brushed against his T-shirt as I walked through the door. All the hairs on my arm stood on end. Inside, I turned to look at him, to see if he'd noticed that I'd touched his shirt, but he was waving to a bunch of guys standing by the trophy cases. He walked over to them without giving me a second glance.

I rubbed the goose bumps on my arm. *Let it happen.*

ALL MORNING at school I kept expecting to run into Austin again, but our schedules were clearly not in sync this year since I didn't see him in the hallway once. Then again, it was only a half day. Maybe he'd take a different path tomorrow when he had to go back to his locker between classes. By ninth period, all the excitement from the start of the day had turned into a discouraged lump in the pit of my stomach. I realized my only hope of seeing Austin was if Hayden invited me to watch the end of football practice after cheerleading. She didn't, and I had to ride the late bus home from school since Sara didn't have a newspaper meeting. When I got home, I was completely worn out from spending the day hoping for something that didn't happen, and Nana was waiting for me at the kitchen table with a peanut-butter-and-banana sandwich.

"I'm not hungry," I said, dropping into the chair next to her and letting my backpack fall at my feet.

"You just don't realize you're hungry," she said, pushing the plate toward me. "Eat."

I picked up one of the sandwich triangles out of habit, then shook my head and put it back down. "Really. I'm not. I had a candy bar from the vending machines after practice."

Nana took the plate away and began triple-wrapping it in Saran wrap. "You always used to want a snack after school," she said with her back to me.

I sighed. "It's not personal, Nana. I'm just not hungry."

I unzipped my backpack and rummaged around. "I have something I need you to sign."

I handed Nana the driver's ed form, and then started looking for a pen. I found one, missing its cap, at the bottom of my bag, but when I sat up to hand it to her, Nana was staring at me with a trembling chin.

She shook her head. "I thought you understood," she said.

Understood?

"When we got the packet last spring," Nana said, "I filed it."

"You mean we already have the form?"

"Yes. I'm saving it for when you are older."

"But fifteen is the age, Nana. Actually, most people sign up as soon as they turn fifteen. Fifteen-and-a-half is late." I stared up at her, confused. She was starting to shake.

"I don't believe in fifteen-year-olds learning to drive. I would like you to wait until you are eighteen." Nana paused and took a deep breath. "Teenagers are terrible drivers, and I will not lose you like I lost your parents."

Her voice cracked on the last word. I braced myself for the guilt I usually felt whenever I made Nana cry, but suddenly I realized that guilt was *not* what I was feeling. Anger made my fingers curl. I wanted to force her hand around the pen and make her sign the form. Practically every fifteen-year-old in the state signed up for driver's ed. Why did *I* have to be different?

"I'd be so careful, Nana. *Please.* I won't be a terrible driver." I wanted to tell her that I wouldn't die in a car accident like my parents had, but I couldn't. Nana's face was crumpling.

"If I lost you, too . . ." Nana didn't finish her sentence. She clutched my paper to her chest and left the room.

I stared at the empty doorway, dumbfounded. It wasn't fair, but how could I argue with her?

I couldn't.

THE NEXT MORNING, Sara parked as far from Austin's spot as possible. I thought she did it on purpose. I craned my neck as we walked toward school, but I couldn't tell if he was hanging out near his car or not. Up ahead, the courtyard was packed. Even though it was only seven-thirty in the morning, the sun warmed my shoulders.

I wore a new turquoise tank top, a denim skirt, and flip-flops, hoping that maybe I'd get another chance to talk to Austin.

And there he was, sitting on the benches fifteen feet in front of me. Lara sat next to him. Austin looked in my direction, so I smiled as I stepped up onto the edge of the courtyard. The tip of my right flip-flop caught on the curb. I tripped and nearly face-planted. I had to take a few jog-steps to catch my balance.

"Are you okay?" Sara asked, grabbing my elbow and trying to steady me.

I stood still for a second and nodded my head without lifting my eyes from the stupid flip-flops. Could I be any more lame? I just hoped Austin wasn't laughing at me.

I took a deep breath and looked up. He was focused on his phone, but Lara's eyes locked with mine as she whispered something to Austin with a wicked smile on her lips. He shrugged and kept thumbing buttons.

My insides crumpled. How dumb could I be? So he noticed me a couple of times. He was still out of my league. *Lara* was the kind of girl he hung out with before school. I straightened up and started walking. The sooner I was inside, away from the scene of my humiliation, the better. I didn't need to stand around and watch Austin not watch me.

As we passed by his group, I noticed Micah sitting on the end of the bench. He waved at me. I waved back, but it took effort to lift my arm.

Sara grabbed my shoulder. "Who is that?" she asked.

"My cousin," I said, sighing. "Micah."

"That's Micah?" She did a double take, and I had to grab her by the arm and pull her forward a couple of steps to get her to stop staring. Sara looked back at him over her shoulder one last time before we went inside.

"He looks different than I expected. He's cute. What was he wearing on his head?"

"It's a religious head-covering," I said. "It's got some weird name. He wears it all the time. The football players call him 'Beanie.' "

Sara stopped by the trophy case and stared straight down her nose at me. "Does Austin call him that?"

I shrugged. "Yeah, but not in a mean way. Lots of players have nicknames. Sometimes they call Sean 'Charmin,' and they call Keith 'Ducky.' "

Sara cut me off. "It's not the same. You seriously like a guy who would make fun of your cousin?"

"Austin doesn't even know we're related."

"Why not?"

"I . . .." I opened and closed my mouth a couple of times because the whole conversation had gotten turned around. "It's never even come up. Besides, it's just a joke. Micah probably doesn't care."

"I doubt that." Sara took a drink from the water fountain as the first bell rang and everyone poured into the building. I needed to go because I had first-period geometry on the opposite side of school.

"See you at lunch?" I asked, hoping she was done yelling at me. It's not as if Austin would stop calling Micah "Beanie" just because he knew we were related, so what difference would it make if he knew?

Sara nodded. "Lunch," she said.

The knot at the back of my neck relaxed as I turned and walked down the hallway to geometry. Sara didn't need to make this into a federal case. If it was an issue, then *Micah* could do something about it. It wasn't my responsibility.

As I PASSED BY the office on my way to lunch, I stopped to stare at the stack of blue driver's ed forms on the tray in the corner. Should I grab another one? I could try to convince Papa to sign it. Part of me really wanted to, but the other part knew I could never be that heartless to Nana. I just wished she'd change her mind— tell me she was happy that I was a cheerleader and that it would be helpful to have another driver in the family. Maybe I would grab a form and keep it in my backpack in case she came around.

Or maybe I'd figure out a way to ask her again, and convince her to say yes.

I was about to head to the cafeteria when I saw Austin, Harrison, Sean, Hayden, and Lara on the other side of the lobby. Lara bumped shoulders with Austin and then put her fingertips on his forearm and laughed at something he said. She seemed so confident. So sure that she had every right to touch him.

Austin waved goodbye to his friends and turned toward me. Why wasn't he going to lunch with them? In a few seconds Austin would see me standing by the doorway to the office. My legs began to shake. Would we talk? I tried to think of something I could say about the team, but then he stopped, glanced over his shoulder, and changed direction. I watched his back as he hurried down the math wing.

I knew I should go join Sara, Zoe, and Skye at our table, but I didn't. I followed Austin, hiding behind clusters of freshmen like I was a spy, in case he turned around and figured out that I was tailing him.

The bell rang for fifth period and the hallway emptied. Now Austin and I were the only ones around. He was about twenty feet ahead of me. If he turned around he'd be able to see me clearly. There was nowhere left to hide. I heard Sara's voice in my head.

If things are so different this year, why are you still stalking him?

I blushed at the imaginary accusation, and decided to cut my losses, turn right at the science hallway, and head back to the cafeteria. Then Austin stopped. He looked around slowly and when his gaze came my way I pretended to be working the combination of the locker in front of me, twisting left, right, left. I tried to pull up on the handle. It didn't work, of course, but I acted all frustrated, like I knew I'd done the combination right.

"Hey!" Someone grabbed my shoulder, and I froze. "That's *my* locker."

A girl I recognized from the basketball team stared down at me. "What are you doing?" she asked.

I gulped and glanced up at the locker number. "Oh!" I looked around, pretending to be confused. "Wrong hallway! Sorry, I thought this was my locker."

She stepped toward me. I could tell she didn't believe my story. I ran off before she could say anything else, but Austin was gone. I quickly walked to the last place I'd seen him. The entrance to the media center?

I pulled the door open and stepped inside. The front desk was empty, but behind it Mrs. Polander was in her office eating lunch. Two guys were sitting at a table playing chess, and in the corner a girl sat hunched over in a study carrel.

Austin stood in front of the magazine rack. I recognized his back. He picked up a copy of *Newsweek* and sat down on one of the blue pleather sofas.

My feet froze where I stood. I couldn't believe I'd actually followed him to the library to watch him read. Lara would say I looked desperate. Sara would say I had no self-respect.

Still, I'd followed Austin plenty of times last year, and he'd never spent his lunch hour in the library. He was usually surrounded by friends. I was curious. I knew I should walk back out the door, meet my friends in the cafeteria, and eat my lunch, but as one foot moved in front of the other I found myself standing right by the magazine rack. I grabbed a *Seventeen* and sat down on the couch next to Austin's. He glanced up at the noise, and when he noticed it was me he smiled.

"Are you a lunchtime reader?" he asked.

What? Did he think I did this every day? "No," I said. "This is my first time."

He smiled even bigger. "Me too," he said, then leaned closer. "Sick of your friends?"

My eyes went wide. "No." What was I supposed to tell him? That I'd followed him? "I had a headache." I rubbed my temple, hoping my lie wasn't completely obvious.

"Oh, sorry," he said, leaning back. "I won't make you talk anymore."

He went back to reading, and I could have smacked myself on the forehead. A whole lunch period alone with Austin and he thought I didn't want to talk. He kicked off his shoes and lay down on the couch with his head against the armrest. I could have run my fingers through his hair, that's how close we were.

I gripped my magazine tightly, inhaled his musky shampoo, and pretended to read silently for the next thirty-four minutes, trying to work up the courage to start the conversation again.

Then the bell rang. Austin and I both stood up and put our magazines back.

"How's your head?" he asked.

"What? Oh, yeah. It's much better."

"Good. Where are you headed?" he asked as we walked out of the library.

"U.S. history."

"I'm this way." He pointed the opposite direction. "I need to get some lunch. Study hall will have to wait. See you around."

He walked off down the hall, and my stomach rumbled. I couldn't believe I'd missed my entire lunch period. Why would Austin skip lunch to read a magazine and then skip study hall to get lunch? He wouldn't be able to eat with his friends. It didn't make any sense.

4

For the rest of the week, Austin's friends ate lunch without him. I wondered if he was going to the library every day, but I couldn't bring myself to check. That would definitely be stalking. Hayden, Lara, Harrison, and Sean were always at their usual table, but without Austin they didn't seem to have much fun. Last year lunchtime always looked like a party. Everyone laughing, flirting, goofing off. Sean would usually do something crazy like stand on a chair and belch at the top of his lungs or pinch some girl's behind as she walked by. And people were always coming over to them to say hi. This year, they just sat at their table and ate, like everyone else in the cafeteria.

I was beginning to think I'd never see Austin again, but then Friday afternoon Hayden invited me to hang out with her before the first football game. She took Lara and me for drive-through coffee, then back to the school parking lot to sit in her car. We still had an hour before Ms. Young expected the cheerleaders; I couldn't figure out why Hayden wanted to be at school so early. Then Austin's Jeep pulled into his spot. Hayden had parked four spaces over. Harrison and Sean were sitting in the car with him. They looked like two bulldogs, a huge one and his slightly smaller sidekick. Austin had the top off, and rap music blared from his stereo.

Hayden squeezed my arm. "Let's go say hi."

I blushed and looked down at my shoes. I barely knew Austin. And I knew Harrison and Sean even less. Why was she asking *me* to go and not Lara?

"I'm not sure this is a good idea," I said to Hayden. My eyes flicked to Lara in the backseat. She snapped her gum.

"Don't worry about me," Lara said. "I couldn't care less who you say hi to."

"Come on," said Hayden, getting out of the car. "He's not going to bite."

As I opened the door, I heard Lara mutter, "Unless you're into that."

"Forget about her," Hayden said, shutting her door. "She's had her chance. Austin just isn't into her."

Nerves wiggled through me as I followed Hayden over to Austin. Lara stayed in the car. All I could think about was last year, when he'd been dating Vi Davison, and then, after they'd broken up, girl after girl. I'd been a complete nobody. Austin wouldn't even have looked at me if I'd smacked into him in the hallway. My neck felt cold. Maybe this was a bad idea. Not just saying hi, but having a crush on Austin in the first place. Hanging out with Hayden. Everything. I was in way over my head.

Hayden draped her arm over the side of the Jeep's door. Austin turned the volume down. "Hey there," he said, smiling at both of us.

I smiled back. Why did Austin have to be so cute? It would be easier to stop breathing than to stop liking him. His shaggy hair hung down over his left eye, and I wanted to reach out and brush it away.

"Are you ready for the game?" he asked me. "It's your first one, right?"

His toffee-brown eyes looked straight at mine. His lips were hypnotizing. First game? Ready?

Hayden poked me in the side. "Uh, yeah," I said. "I think I'm ready."

Just then Aunt Shelli's red minivan pulled up next to us. "Hi, Essie!" she called as Micah climbed out of the car.

I waved to her, but I could sense everyone wondering how I knew Beanie's mom.

She held up a bright orange crossing-guard vest. "You sure you won't wear this?" she called to Micah. "Nana went to a lot of trouble to get it for you."

"I'll be fine." Micah scowled. "Goodbye."

Aunt Shelli hesitated, then put the vest on the passenger seat. "Have a great game, everyone," she said, then drove away.

"Hey," Micah said to us when she was gone. "What's going on?"

No one answered. Even under normal circumstances it would have been hard for Micah to just ease into the group after stepping out of his mom's red minivan. But then there was the safety vest.

"Dude, why did your mom want you to wear that jacket?" Sean asked.

Everyone started laughing, and two big red splotches broke out on Micah's cheeks.

"Does she want you to wear it during the game?" Harrison added.

Micah shook his head and the splotches got even darker, until they were almost purple. "She wanted me to wear it after the game. When I walk home. There's no sidewalk, and she's worried that drivers won't see me in the dark."

"Do you need a ride home?" Austin asked. "I could give you a lift."

My stomach squeezed. I didn't want Micah telling everyone the reason he was walking. They already thought he was strange enough.

"Thanks for the offer," said Micah, "but I'm good."

Austin gave Micah a look. I hadn't wanted him to explain, but without giving a reason, it sounded like Micah was just being rude. Why would anyone choose to walk home after a football game when the captain was offering him a ride?

But what was better, rude or weird? Lara was staring at us. It gave me chills. I tried to keep my eyes on Austin's car, but her eyes bored into me.

"Do you want to grab a bite at Amir's after the game?" Hayden asked everyone.

"I can't," Micah said, even though it was kind of obvious Hayden wasn't really inviting *him*.

"I'm not sure," said Austin. "Are you going?" he asked me.

Disbelief. Austin wanted to know if I was going.

"You have to come." Hayden nodded at me.

"Sure," I said. "Sounds fun." Then I remembered Sara, Zoe, and Skye were coming to the game to watch me cheer. Zoe had mentioned something about pizza afterward, but we didn't have definite plans. I was sure they'd understand why I said yes to Austin.

"What about you?" Hayden poked Harrison in the chest.

He was staring at Micah with wrinkled eyebrows, as if Micah was a math problem that didn't make any sense. "Yeah. I'll be there," Harrison answered.

"Uh, I'll see you guys inside," Micah said. He jogged away to the gym entrance; he couldn't leave fast enough.

"What was that about?" Sean asked. "Do we smell or something?" He sniffed his armpit.

"Does he even want to be on the team?" Harrison asked. "He should at least try to be one of us." That's what I'd been saying to Micah the other day.

Austin shrugged and said, "Maybe we should all start wearing little hats."

Or Micah should take his off.

Harrison and Sean laughed and grabbed their bags from the back of the Jeep.

"See you after the game," Austin told Hayden. Then he turned to me. "Bye." The look he gave me seemed to last a little longer than the one he gave Hayden. But maybe I was imagining things.

"Bye," I said, wishing I knew if his look had been real.

When they were gone, Hayden and I went back to her car. We still had an hour before cheerleader pregame stuff.

"Took you long enough," Lara said as Hayden turned on the engine.

Hayden ignored her and put the car in gear. "I was right. Austin *is* into you," she told me. My heart skittered. Did that mean I wasn't imagining things?

"He's always into somebody," Lara said. "Wait five minutes and he'll be interested in someone else."

My eyes pricked. Lara was just trying to hurt my feelings, but Sara would have said the same thing. Only maybe in a nicer way.

"That's not true." Hayden tossed her ponytail. "He dated me for a whole month."

My mouth fell open. He dated Hayden?

"Don't worry. It was a million years ago, when we were sophomores. We never even did it."

I smiled and nodded my head. For a moment I wished I'd stayed in dance troupe, or even joined newspaper, like Sara had wanted. In over my head didn't even begin to describe this situation.

Lara grabbed my headrest and pulled herself forward so she could speak right in my ear. "You'd be better off with Beanie," she said. "I'm sure *he'd* stick around. Kind of like a leech."

Hayden laughed. "Did you see what his mom wanted him to wear? I do not know how he made the football team. He's more science club. . . . Or newspaper!"

I turned my head and looked out the window so they couldn't see my face. I knew I'd had the same thoughts about Micah, but it made me feel uncomfortable to hear *them* say it. I tried to shake the feeling off. Maybe he'd change his mind and try to blend in.

As GAME TIME got closer, I was too excited to spend any more time thinking about Micah or Lara. When the team ran out on the field, my thoughts were only on football. And Austin. Cheering at an actual game was just like I'd imagined. My blood rushed from the way the crowd screamed. Nana and Papa were right in the front row. I couldn't believe Nana had bought herself booster pompoms! When we did our sideline dance, the music from the speakers was so loud it felt like a drummer was sitting inside my chest. We won, 14–0.

After the game, Hayden offered to drive me to Amir's. She was in a hurry, so I didn't have time to find Sara and tell everyone where I was going. I sent her a quick text message. I barely had time to say hello to my grandparents.

Amir's was *the* hangout spot, but the owner of the diner gave us a dirty look as we trampled in. His bushy brows furrowed as he grunted at us and nodded toward a bunch of tables pushed together in the back. We *were* kind of loud, but I loved the way everyone in the restaurant turned to look at us. Like we were celebrities.

"I have a good feeling about this season," Sean said to Austin.

Austin sat right across from me. He folded his arms across his chest and stretched his legs out. If I slid my feet forward the tiniest bit our toes would touch.

"Our defense rocks," Sean added.

Austin picked up his menu and scanned the items. "I guess."

"I think we could make it to quarterfinals at least," said Sean. "As long as we go further than last year, I'll be happy."

"It's all about controlling the game," said Harrison. "I can't make so many mistakes. I need to execute."

"You played fine," Austin said, looking at the ceiling.

A tired-looking waitress came by and asked Austin if we were ready to order. He told her we needed another minute, then caught me staring at him over the top of my menu as the waitress walked away. The blood rushed to my cheeks, and I pulled my menu higher to compose myself. Austin tapped my foot with his, and I met his gaze.

"What are you going to order?" he asked. The way his toffee eyes held mine when he asked the question was so different from the way anyone else would ever ask it. The eye contact was intense, as though he really wanted to know the answer. To know even more than the answer. I put my menu down.

"I can't decide between French fries and a sundae." I shrugged and fingered my napkin.

"It's a tough decision." He smiled. "I think I'm going to get something I've never ordered before. Do you think the pineapple shake is any good?"

I didn't know if he was flirting with me or not, but I couldn't think of anything to say either way. I looked down at my hands. Without realizing it, I'd torn my napkin in half.

Just then, Wyatt and Eric walked over to our table.

"Hey, Austin. Harrison," Wyatt said. "Good game."

"Thanks," said Harrison.

"Not going to win you any scholarships, though, huh?" Eric said.

Harrison's face turned as red as his hair. "I'm pacing myself. We've still got a whole season to play."

Eric grabbed two chairs from an empty table nearby and said to Hayden, "Scoot over."

Hayden glanced at Austin and raised her eyebrows, like she was waiting for him to do something. His foot was still touching mine. He held my eyes for a second more, and I got the feeling that he really didn't want to get involved in whatever was happening at the table, but he sighed and turned toward Wyatt and Eric.

"It's too crowded here, guys," he said.

Wyatt just stood there for a second, but Eric shot Austin a dirty look, left the chairs in the middle of the floor, and stormed out. Wyatt followed.

When the waitress returned I ordered a side of fries, but once they arrived I couldn't eat any of them. Every cell in my body was focused on one thing. Austin.

"Guess you should have gotten ice cream," he said.

My cheeks twitched in a half-smile. "I guess I should have gotten ice cream," I repeated.

What was wrong with me? What was I doing here? I didn't know how to handle myself with these people. I'd barely spoken a word, and the ones I had spoken were idiotic. At least Lara was at the other end of the table—she couldn't hear me.

Finally, the waitress brought us the check and stood over our table like she really wanted us to clear out. As we left, Hayden invited everyone to come back to her place. She told me that her parents were cool with her having parties; that they liked being the hangout house. But it was already ten-fifty, and my curfew was eleven. I hoped Hayden wouldn't be annoyed at having to drop me off first.

Suddenly I felt a hand on my shoulder.

"Do you need to get home?" Austin asked. "I could give you a ride."

Dumbstruck, I nodded. Austin hadn't moved his hand, and I wanted to enjoy the feeling, but I couldn't. It wasn't as if Austin was taking me home at the end of the night; he was taking me home before the fun even started. Like a kid who needed a babysitter.

"My grandparents are probably waiting up for me," I explained, then realized that made me seem even younger.

"You guys coming?" Hayden put her arms around both of us, as if Austin and I were a couple. Austin gave me a slow smile before he looked back at Hayden.

"I'm going to take Essie home," Austin told her. "Maybe I'll swing by later."

Hayden pouted. "You're never around anymore," she said to him. Then she turned to me. "Next time ask if you can stay out later. We hang at my house every week."

I nodded at her but didn't answer. My mouth was dry. Reality had finally hit me. I was about to spend five minutes in Austin's car. With him. Alone.

My knees started knocking. I had always thought that was just an expression. But I was trying so hard to keep my body from shaking that the rattling was escaping through my kneecaps. I took a deep breath and hoped that I would be able to think of one non-idiotic thing to say on the way home.

We climbed in the car and Austin asked, "Where do you live?"

"Off of Inkster. 1214 Birch Trail."

He pulled out of the parking lot. "Do you live with your grand-parents?"

"Yes. My parents died when I was three."

"Oh." He was quiet for a minute. "Sorry. I didn't know that. That must be rough."

"I love my grandparents," I said. "They're great—" I stopped. I couldn't believe what I'd been about to say. I'd never said it out loud before. Not even to Sara.

"It sounded like you were going to say something else," Austin said. He reached over and gave my hand a squeeze. "You can tell me if you want."

I swallowed, touching my hand where he'd squeezed it. "They really are great," I repeated, "but sometimes they don't feel much like parents. You can fight with parents. They might be overpro-tective, but it's just because they're trying to help you grow up to be a good person. With my grandparents, I sometimes feel like they're trying to *stop* me from growing up, from figuring out who I am. They want me to stay their little granddaughter forever."

"Wow," Austin said. "That would be hard. I know it's not the same, but sometimes I feel like my parents expect me to be just like my older brother. And everyone at school wants me to be a certain way, too."

I nodded. "You're like a school celebrity."

Austin groaned. "That's a terrible thing to say."

I bit my bottom lip. Just when things had been going so well, it figured I'd say something dumb. "Sorry," I said. "I meant it as a compliment." When Austin pulled into my driveway, I grabbed the door handle. I needed to get out of the car before I embarrassed myself further. "Thanks for the ride."

"Just a second." He put his hand on my arm. "You're going to take off so quickly after insulting me?"

"Uh . . ." Was he really that mad? The corners of his mouth were tilting up.

"I mean, I thought I was more than just a *school* celebrity," he said. "Doesn't the whole district know about me?"

I smacked my forehead. "You're right. They do! I think all of southeastern Michigan has heard of you."

Austin's smile grew, and I let go of the door handle. He slid his fingers down my arm until we were holding hands.

"You're a sophomore, right?"

I nodded.

"And you made varsity cheerleading?"

"I've taken dance my whole life," I said, drawing a shaky breath. "Modern, jazz, hip-hop, and tap dance. Mostly tap. I guess it helped."

"Tap dance? Like Shirley Temple?"

Instantly, I started babbling. "Yeah, that was my grandmother's dream. Not mine. I'm not the only sophomore, though. Christine Kowalski is in tenth grade, too. I don't dance anymore. I still love it, though."

Austin touched one of my curls, and I stopped talking. He

twisted the end around his finger. "You're the only girl I know with hair like this."

I wrinkled my nose. "I always wanted straight and shiny shampoo-commercial hair."

"No," he said. "I like it."

Austin pulled my head forward gently until our mouths were only inches apart. His cologne made me dizzy, and when I closed my eyes, his lips pressed against mine, soft and warm, lingering for a few seconds. Suddenly it was as if my entire being was paying attention to what would happen next.

I opened my eyes. Austin grinned at me in a way that made me want to dance. My chest hollowed out, and I smiled back just as the porch lights from my house flicked on.

"I think my grandparents want me to go inside," I said.

He cleared his throat. "I guess so."

"Night." We both said it at the same time.

I climbed out of the car and watched from the doorway of my house as his black Jeep backed out of my driveway. My lips still felt warm and tingly and alive. My life was finally starting.

5

I didn't like Austin the first time I saw him. I mean, I thought he was cute, but nothing more than that. Then my feelings completely changed one day last February. I was hurrying down the social studies wing, late for world civ, when I saw Austin and Vi huddled in the doorway of an empty classroom. She was crying, and he was comforting her. He brushed a few tears off her cheek with his thumb and then kissed her forehead. She laid her head on his shoulder. As I passed by, hoping that they wouldn't notice me, I couldn't stop staring. Suddenly I realized I wanted to be the girl with her head on Austin's shoulder. The feeling was overwhelming. Austin and Vi broke up a week later. And I'd been fantasizing about becoming his new girlfriend ever since.

Sara believed all the rumors about their breakup, that it was because Vi wouldn't go all the way with Austin. She never failed to remind me that Vi had been completely ostracized by the cheerleaders and football players for the rest of the school year, even though she was a senior and Austin only a junior.

When Nana dropped me off at Sara's house the next day, I

wasn't exactly sure how Sara would take the news that Austin and I had kissed. When I got there, she was wearing an apron that said QUICHE THE COOK. All the ingredients for her sinfully decadent triple chocolate cake sat on the kitchen counter.

"I didn't know if you were coming," she said. "I just started. Here."

Sara shoved an apron at me that looked like it came from the *I Love Lucy* show. I tied it on and said, "Why wouldn't I be here?"

She shrugged. "Flour," she said, holding out her hand like a surgeon.

I handed her the dusty bag and took a deep breath. "Austin drove me home last night."

Sara scooped two cups of flour into the bowl, carefully leveling each one, before turning to me. "You mean last night when you blew us off?"

I flinched. She had texted back "Fine."

"You're angry?"

"First you drop dancing, next you ditch your friends?"

They weren't the same at all. "I wasn't ditching you guys. I was . . ."

Everything seemed to make sense last night, but now Sara had me all confused. "I'm really sorry."

Sara measured the baking powder, and I felt myself shrinking. I hated disappointing people. "I would never ditch you. I didn't realize that's what I was doing. I was just so excited to be with Austin. Please forgive me."

Sara sighed. "Okay. I forgive you," she said. "Butter." She held out her hand.

I gave her a stick of butter. She mixed in silence, and I wondered if I could tell her more about Austin. Even though she said she'd forgiven me, the air still felt tense between us. She finally broke the silence.

"He drove you home?"

Thank goodness, because I couldn't keep the news inside for one more second. "He kissed me good night."

"Sugar," she said.

I didn't expect her to scream and jump up and down for me, but she could have at least asked for more details. I handed her another sack. "You might pretend to be excited. Or even interested."

Sara filled the measuring cup, then held it up like she was making a toast. "Hurray for you. Yay. The biggest male slut in the school kissed you!"

I wanted to take back everything I'd told her. I grabbed the sack of flour and started making tiny rips all along the top edge of the paper bag.

"You are so hypocritical," I finally said. "If somebody called a girl a slut just because she'd had a lot of boyfriends, you'd think it was horrible."

"Okay, he's not a slut." She dumped another cup of sugar in the bowl. "He's a player. I don't want you to get hurt."

"Maybe I won't get hurt. Maybe he actually likes me. Is that too impossible for you to believe?"

"Essie, don't be that way. Baking soda." When I didn't move, Sara reached around me for the orange box. "He'd be crazy not to like you."

I shrugged and looked away. I shouldn't have told her.

"Salt."

I went to the table without handing her the container and got out my homework. Sara finished mixing the ingredients by herself and put the cake pan in the oven. I wanted to make her take me home, but I didn't want to speak to her. I wished I could drive myself.

Sara put the mixing bowl in the sink, but kept the spoon and licked the batter off it.

"Is he a good kisser?"

I looked at her out of the corner of my eye. I wasn't going to answer a pity question.

"I'm sorry." She gave a sheepish grin. "I really want to know. Is he a good kisser?"

The scent of baking chocolate wafted through the kitchen. It reminded me of the hundreds of other days we'd spent here baking and having fun. I inhaled deeply, my senses flashing back to the warmth of Austin's lips. "Even better than in my imagination."

Sara was wrong. He wasn't playing me. His kiss wouldn't have felt so amazing if he didn't truly like me.

AUSTIN'S KISS was all I could think about for the rest of the long Labor Day weekend, his kiss and everything that could actually happen now. Austin calling me at the end of every day to say good night. Austin walking me to class and holding my hand. Austin telling me how much he liked me.

I wondered if Nana would be able to see that I'd changed, that I was no longer a girl-who'd-never-been-kissed, but she treated me the same as ever, even down to the Mickey Mouse–shaped pancake she made me for breakfast, and the carrot muffin she snuck into my backpack so that I wouldn't buy junk food after cheerleading.

The weather for Tuesday afternoon's practice was perfect, sunny with a light breeze, and Ms. Young let us practice outside. We spread out in small groups and started stretching. The air smelled like freshly mowed lawn, and my insides were all jittery because as soon as the football team came outside I'd see Austin. I'd only seen him once that day, in the hallway. He smiled at me, but we hadn't talked since our kiss. I'd sort of been expecting him to call me over the weekend, but he must have lost his school directory.

"Ladies," Ms. Young called out after we'd finished stretching. "Last week was sloppy! Our sidelines need to be perfect this week, and we only have three more practices until the next game. I want 'Purple and Gold' five times, then 'Panthers Can't Be Beat.' Eyes on Hayden!"

We lined up in two rows of nine, and went through those cheers, then four others, over and over again. I wondered if Austin would offer to drive me home again Friday night. Sweat poured down my face and neck. Where had the breeze gone?

"One more time," shouted Ms. Young. "Essie, focus! You're all over the place today!"

We did "Purple and Gold" again. From across the soccer field where we practiced, I noticed the football players run out onto their field for laps. I tried to pick out Austin, but I was too far away, or maybe he wasn't on the field yet.

"Essie!" Ms. Young shouted at me again. I turned back to the squad, but no one was left. They'd split up into four groups and spread out over the grass.

"If you daydream like that when we're stunting, you could break your neck!" Ms. Young was strict about safety.

I nodded my head to let her know that I'd do better, and ran over to Hayden. She was waiting for me with Gabi and Jess, two of the juniors on the squad.

"All right, let's see a half-liberty into a twist out," Ms. Young called.

I was a flyer, the girl who went up in the air and trusted her teammates not to let her fall. I tried to put Austin out of my mind, but before Hayden and Gabi lifted me up Hayden whispered, "So, what happened Friday night?"

A smile burst out on my face. It would feel so good to tell someone who would be excited for me. "We talked in my driveway for about five minutes and he kissed me good night."

I put my foot into her hands and jumped up and around. Jess steadied my back leg while I raised my knee and lifted my right arm to a high V. Then they tossed me up. I crossed my legs and twisted my body around as I fell into their cradled arms, and they popped me back on the ground. The rush of flying made my blood pump faster.

"You guys make such a cute couple," Hayden whispered again when I was back on the ground. "What happened after the kiss?"

"That was it," I said.

"You can tell me." Hayden pouted. "Austin never came by

my house, so I figured you guys were having fun. Don't keep secrets."

"No. That was it. Really. My grandmother turned on the porch lights and I went inside."

I couldn't tell if Hayden believed me or not, but what did she think we'd done? I mean, we'd barely had three conversations. A kiss was plenty.

Ms. Young shouted for another half-liberty. Mine especially had still been kind of wobbly. When we finished she yelled, "Good practice. Everyone take two laps around the field, and you're done."

Hayden didn't ask me any more questions. In fact, she didn't say anything more to me at all.

WHEN I GOT HOME from practice, Nana sprang the news on me. She'd invited Micah over for dinner so we could have more time to get to know each other. When he arrived at around six-thirty, dinner wasn't ready yet, so Nana suggested we do our homework at the kitchen table until it was done. Which meant she'd be watching us the entire time. But there was no other place to work. The dining-room table was already set for dinner.

"How are your classes so far?" I asked as I unpacked my bags.

"Pretty good," he said. "Pershing has a lot more AP classes than my old high school." Micah pulled a spiral notebook, a giant graphing calculator, and a math book out of his bag. "Nana, do you have a pencil I could borrow?" he asked.

"Of course, sugar," Nana said. She went into the office and came back with four pencils and an electric pencil sharpener.

"Thanks," Micah said. He began to sharpen one of the pencils, then whispered to me so Nana couldn't hear. "Maybe she thought I'd have to do a four-limbed problem?" He pointed at all the pencils.

I smiled. "Or she brought one for writing and three for chewing?"

Micah popped a pencil between his teeth like a rose stem, and began working on his math homework. I had to read a chapter in my chemistry book. We sat studying side by side for a while as Nana hummed to herself and put the finishing touches on dinner. My mind kept wandering away from my reading.

One on one, Micah wasn't really that weird at all. Other than the kippah, you wouldn't even know he was Jewish. He was nice and funny, actually. I hoped the guys on the team would start to see that soon. When he took a break from his homework to crack his knuckles, I whispered to him impulsively, "When I was little, I used to wish that you were my big brother."

Micah wrinkled his eyebrows and shot me a curious look. Then he stole a glance at Nana and seemed to relax when he saw that she wasn't listening to us. "Why did you say that?" he asked.

I bit my lip. I'd obviously dumped way too much information on him. He probably thought I was a stalker-cousin now. "It was just something silly I used to imagine when I was little. I don't know why I mentioned it. I thought it was funny. Forget I said anything." I waved my hand, wishing I could flick my words away.

"No," Micah said. "I'm glad you told me." He looked at Nana again, then lowered his voice even further. "I used to . . . I used to imagine what it would be like if you were my sister, too."

"Wow," I said, a chill zipping down my back. "That's a coincidence."

Micah looked at me for a long time before answering. "Or something else."

"What do you mean?" I tried to search Micah's face for clues, but he wouldn't meet my eyes.

"I think you should ask Nana about that. Or Papa."

"Ask Nana what?" Suddenly, Nana was standing right next to me. I nearly jumped out of my chair. I hadn't noticed her and had no idea how much she'd heard. She held out a wooden spoon filled with tomato sauce. "I wanted to see if the sauce was to your liking," she said to Micah.

Micah took a taste and gave Nana a thumbs-up. "It's delicious."

Nana nodded. "Good. And your question?" she asked me.

"Uh . . ." My brain was scrambled. Something told me that telling Nana the truth wasn't a good idea. That it was a topic that might make her cry or worse. "I wanted to know when dinner will be ready. I'm starving."

Micah raised his eyebrows at me, and Nana looked at me like she knew I had something else on my mind. "Dinner's ready right now," she finally said. Maybe she could sense the danger in the real question, too. "Pack up your homework."

I bugged my eyes out at Micah as I put my book away. Nana carried the food into the dining room.

"Sorry," Micah said. "I didn't mean to put you in an uncomfortable position."

"You can make it up to me by telling me what you meant." Nana called us to the table from the other room. "Later," I added.

After dinner, which was mostly Papa talking to Micah about football, I walked Micah to the door. Nana and Papa were in the kitchen doing the dishes, so we wouldn't be overheard again.

"Okay, now. Why wasn't it a coincidence?"

Micah looked uncomfortable. "I shouldn't have said anything."

"But you did. You have to tell me." I was starting to imagine all kinds of crazy things. Was I a love child? Was Micah?

Micah scratched the side of his head. "Let me think about it, okay?"

I folded my arms across my chest. I'd buried any curiosity I had about our two families a long time ago, but Micah's words had reignited it. I didn't want to wait.

Micah opened the door. "I have to go," he said.

Obviously I wasn't going to get any more information today. "Okay," I mumbled.

Micah walked out halfway and paused. "Can I tell you something else that's probably not my business? About Austin. Be careful."

Hearing Austin's name made me all jittery, but I tried to act casual. "What are you talking about?" I'd never told Micah anything about Austin. "Why would you say that?"

"I overheard some guys on the team talking about you. About Friday night after the game."

"Was one of them Austin?" It couldn't be. I knew it, but my shoulders tensed anyway.

He shook his head. "No. Not Austin."

I breathed a sigh of relief. "I don't care if stupid people have nothing better to do than make stuff up. That doesn't mean Austin's a bad guy." My jaw clenched. Part of me wished Micah hadn't told me. If I wanted to hear someone bash Austin, I'd hang out with Sara. "Wait a minute. Did you say anything? Like, stick up for me? Did you tell them you're my cousin?" I knew I should be worried about what people were saying I did with Austin, but suddenly I felt more worried that they'd be talking about what Austin did with Beanie's cousin.

"No," he said, looking at me like he'd heard my thoughts.

Shame burned my ears. We'd had a really nice night together. How could I still feel embarrassed by him? "It's okay if you did," I lied.

"I didn't. I wasn't part of the conversation."

"I had a nice time hanging out tonight," I offered.

"Yeah. Me too," he said, but his voice didn't sound like he meant it. "See you later," he added, then headed to his car.

I closed the door, trying to decide which I felt more, guilt or relief.

BY WEDNESDAY MORNING, my post-kiss excitement had worn off and turned into post-kiss fear. Maybe that kiss would turn out to be the sum total of my sort-of relationship with Austin. The most I'd ever get. I'd thought it was just the beginning, but Austin hadn't called me or spoken to me or done anything more than smile and wave when I passed him in the hallway again just after first period. I thought something had changed between us with that kiss, but he wasn't acting that way at all.

It was agony. I dreaded going to cheerleading practice after school and having Hayden ask me how things were going with Austin. I could just see Lara's eyebrow lifting when I said that things weren't. And of course I couldn't say anything to Sara. There wasn't any point. I knew exactly what she'd say. That this is what Austin did: used girls and moved on. That I was lucky all we'd done was kiss, even though clearly there were people thinking we'd done more.

I couldn't face Sara and Zoe and Skye. I didn't want to pretend I wasn't thinking about Austin. At lunch I bailed on them. I'd go read a magazine instead.

And maybe I'd run into Austin again.

I was practically hyperventilating when I opened the media center door, but the pleather couches were empty. The chess players were at their table. And the girl was still scribbling away in her study carrel. Mrs. Polander sat behind the circulation desk.

Maybe Austin was running late. I grabbed a magazine and sat down on the sofa facing the door, my eyes shifting between the magazine and the doorway. And then Micah walked in. He came over as soon as he noticed me.

"Hey," he said. "What are you doing here?"

I didn't want to be rude, but I also didn't want to be talking to Micah when Austin showed up. Also, Micah's kippah had slipped off to the side of his head. A clip kept it from falling, but the awkward angle did not help him look less weird.

"I have a headache," I said. It had backfired as an excuse with Austin, but I hoped it was a way to get Micah to leave me alone without him taking it personally. "I wanted to sit somewhere quiet."

"Oh," he said, settling down on the couch next to me. "I just got tired of eating lunch with people who don't really want me around."

I'd seen Micah eating with some of the junior football players. I'd assumed he was making friends. I guessed I could have asked him to sit with me. I hadn't even thought of that.

Micah cracked the spine of his book and started reading. I pretended to read, too, eyes still drawn to the media center entrance, but now I wasn't sure if I wanted Austin to show up. What would he think if he saw me spending my lunch here with Micah? The kid no one wanted to eat with. I should have just gone to the cafeteria.

"Essie," Micah whispered. I looked over at him. Maybe my face looked annoyed. "Sorry," he said. He rubbed his forehead.

"No. It's okay." I put down my magazine.

"I need you to do something for me."

My shoulders tensed. "What?"

"Eric and Wyatt are going to let Austin take some hits on Friday. On purpose. You need to tell him."

"Are you sure? Why would they do that? He could get hurt." I pictured Austin lying on the football field doubled over in pain.

Micah nodded. "That's the point. Eric is pissed at him."

"But we'll lose."

"We're playing one of the top teams in the state. We're not going to win. They figure it doesn't matter whether we lose by 20 or 40."

My eyes darted around the media center, as if anyone associated with the football team would actually be lurking nearby. "But why do you want *me* to tell Austin?" I asked. "*You* should tell him."

"You obviously know him better than I do." Micah's cheeks turned pink. "The seniors on the team don't really like me. I try to stay out of their way."

Oh.

Micah upset his dad and bent the rules of his religion just to play football. I wondered if he was sorry since the players his own age barely tolerated him and the older players liked him even less. I studied his face, trying to see what the football players saw, to understand why he couldn't be one of them. The kippah? It had to be more than that.

"Okay," I said. "I'll try to talk to him, but I don't really know him that well."

The bell rang and I trudged out of the library after Micah with the vaguely nauseated feeling of having too much unwanted information. Lara stepped out of the girls' bathroom across the hall. She stopped when she saw Micah and me, and looked back and forth between us, a smile on her lips like she knew some private joke.

"You two are perfect for each other," she said in a sticky-sweet voice. She stepped past us to her locker, but I could see that she was still watching us out of the corner of her eye.

I turned to Micah, ashamed. That she acted like we were a couple. That she didn't know we were cousins. That I still didn't really want anyone to know.

"I'm this way," I said, taking off down the science hallway, not even looking back to see if Micah had gone his own way or was still standing there alone.

6

For the next two days, I thought and thought about how I could tell Austin what Micah had told me. Go up to him in the hallway? Call him at night? Nothing felt right. Whatever I did, he'd probably think I was throwing myself at him, and he clearly wasn't interested in getting to know me further.

But I couldn't let my fear of rejection put him at risk, so on Friday I stuck around after school hoping I could talk to Austin in the parking lot. He was never alone though, so I hid in the entryway of the girls' locker room until the team finished their pregame meeting and the coaches went back to their office. The players walked by me on their way to the boys' locker room. Micah straggled at the end of the pack. I took a deep breath, wiped my sweaty palms on my cheerleading skirt, and whispered his name loudly as he passed.

Micah whipped his head around. "Essie? What are you doing here?" His eyes widened in surprise.

"I haven't had a chance to talk to Austin yet." I rubbed my hands on my skirt again, and bit my lip.

"It's been two days," he whispered, looking over his shoulder. "Everyone's in game mode now."

"There was never a time to talk to him. I told you I didn't know him that well," I whispered back. For instance, I didn't know if he'd treat me like a leper if I tried to talk to him.

Micah sighed. "I'll see if I can get him." He went into the locker room.

I chewed on a fingernail. I'd mostly outgrown the habit except for when I was really nervous. Would Austin be mad at me for interrupting? Would he act like we'd never kissed? It would be so much worse to go back to being nothing to him now.

I moved out into the hallway, and I could hear noises from the locker room. Some guys whistling but others grumbling.

"Keep your chicks in line, King," somebody said. "This is football time."

When Austin stepped through the door, I couldn't meet his eyes. Did he think I was desperate? I stared at his cleats instead. "Sorry," I said. "I didn't mean to cause trouble."

"It's no trouble," he said. "Don't worry."

I looked up at him. He wore his purple jersey and gold pants, and the thick lines of grease on his cheeks made his eyes even warmer than usual. The hallway and locker room slipped away; nothing existed but his face.

"Came to wish me good luck?" He was joking, but also confused. Why *was* I there? Even the players' *girlfriends* didn't interrupt before games.

"Uh, sure," I said, trying to remember what I was supposed to say. How could he be smiling at me? I nearly lost my ability to speak. "I need to tell you something. It's going to sound weird."

"Weird could be good." Austin grinned.

Was he flirting with me? After ignoring me for a week? I knew I should be angry. Sara's words echoed in my brain. *He's a player.* But my chest throbbed with hope. Maybe he still liked me. I tried to concentrate. I had to tell him about the game.

"Someone told me Eric and Wyatt might not defend you tonight. They're pissed."

His smile faded. "Is this a joke?"

I shook my head.

He ran his fingers through his hair, then tilted his head and stared at me hard. "How do you know?"

I shifted my feet. "Just from around."

"From around?" Austin looked like he was waiting for me to say more, but there was nothing more I could tell him.

He rubbed the heel of his hand into his forehead. He looked so stressed out I felt like I'd caused the problem. "Maybe you should tell Coach Ryan?" I said.

"I'm not going to rat out a teammate. Besides, I don't have any proof." Austin squeezed and unsqueezed his fist. I closed my eyes, trying to think of something that would help. Something that Eric and Wyatt might care about more than getting revenge.

"What if you told them there's a recruiter in the stands? Wyatt can't wait to play for a scout. He'd never throw the game then."

"King! Are you still playing tonight?" somebody shouted from the locker room.

"Coming," Austin called, but he was looking at me funny.

"What?" I asked, tucking a curl behind my ears. My hair was always trying to escape.

"Nothing." Austin stared at me like something was different, but he couldn't tell what it was. "You just surprise me," he finally said. "From the way Hayden talks about you, I keep picturing you differently, but you're nothing like your friends."

At first I thought he meant Sara, Zoe, and Skye when he said "your friends." I couldn't figure out how he knew them. Then I realized he meant Hayden and Lara. They were the ones I wasn't like. My shoulders drooped. It was so obvious I didn't belong in his world. "Oh," I said.

"Hey. I meant that in a good way." He stood up straighter. "What are you doing tomorrow night?"

My voice stuck in my throat. He might be asking me out, but he might be making small talk. I couldn't tell him I was doing nothing. I'd look like I had no plans. Which was true, but I didn't want him to know that. Besides, I almost always wound up doing something with Sara. I bit my lip. "I haven't decided yet," I said.

"See a movie with me."

"King!" a voice shouted.

"I have to go," Austin said, backing into the locker room. "Tomorrow. Seven o'clock."

I took a deep breath and said, "Okay."

Austin disappeared and I realized my hands were shaking. This was the biggest thing that had ever happened to me. So why did I hear Sara's voice in my head telling me I was being completely naïve?

———

JUST BEFORE the fourth quarter, Coach Ryan called a time-out. The cheerleaders jumped up and led the crowd in "Panthers Can't Be Beat" and "Go Panthers." It was easy to get the fans going. I felt the excitement, too, like pom-poms shaking in my chest. For three solid quarters, Pershing had dominated. Almost every player, including Eric and Wyatt, was having the best game of his life. They hadn't let a single pass rusher close to Austin. We were beating Washington 27–3.

When the game was over, Pershing fans were electrified. No one had expected us to win, and everyone was talking about how the team had been on fire. I wondered if it was because Austin told his teammates a recruiter was watching.

After the game, a huge group from our school celebrated in the parking lot. Austin found me standing by the gym door, waiting for Nana and Papa.

"Are you going to Hayden's?"

"I hadn't been planning on it," I answered. Hayden hadn't mentioned it lately and I wasn't sure if I was still invited.

"You should come," he said. "I'll give you a ride."

Another ride! "I'll have to ask my grandparents," I said.

He smiled. "Meet me at my car."

Nana, of course, didn't see why I had to go out after every game. It was too much, too tiring for me, she worried. Finally I told them it was my responsibility as a cheerleader to celebrate with the team, and Papa said I could go. Nana wouldn't give me a later curfew, though. I still had to be home at eleven.

———

HARRISON AND AUSTIN were waiting in the Jeep. I climbed into the backseat, and Austin gave me his varsity jacket for the ride because the top was off his car. I wasn't cold, but I took it because I loved the idea of wearing something of Austin's. As we pulled out of the parking lot, Harrison made a noise that sounded like a growl.

Austin laughed, but it sounded stiff. "Feeling good?"

"I crushed skulls tonight!" Harrison smacked his palm against the dashboard. "Yeah!" he shouted again. A couple of guys in the parking lot shouted back. "Pershing rocks!"

Austin honked his horn in celebration, then turned the car onto Pershing Road. The street was empty, so he gave it some gas. Out of nowhere we saw somebody walking not too far ahead of us. Austin slammed on the brakes. The guy jumped off to the side of the road and fell down. We pulled to a stop as whoever it was stood up and dusted himself off.

Micah.

"Are you okay?" I asked, grabbing onto the roll bar. I wanted to jump out and help him, but he was already up.

"Sorry, man. I didn't see you." Austin kept blinking his eyes like he was hoping this was all happening in his imagination. "Did I hurt you?"

"No, no. It's just a scrape," Micah said, rubbing his elbow. "Guess I should have worn that vest." He laughed halfheartedly.

"Are you sure you're all right?" I asked again.

"I'm fine," Micah said, but he wouldn't look at me. "Great game," he told Austin.

Austin nodded. "I played okay. Harrison rocked, though."

"Yeah." Micah said. "Good game."

"Thanks," Harrison said. "It feels different when you *know* a scout is watching."

Micah shrugged. "Do you really think a scout was there? Wouldn't we have seen him?"

"They don't wear neon signs," Harrison said.

Micah's eyes flickered over to Austin and then back to Harrison. Then he looked at me. I couldn't tell what he was thinking. But I wished he'd start making more of an effort. Why not pretend there was a scout, even if he didn't quite believe it?

"I should go." Micah picked his bag up from the dirt.

"You sure you don't want a lift?" Austin asked. "We've got room for one more."

"No, thanks."

"Bye," I called as Austin put the car in gear and pulled back onto the road.

I took a deep breath, looked over my shoulder, and watched Micah walking. A bit farther from the road this time. When I turned back around, I saw Harrison staring at him, too.

"I don't get that kid," he said to me, shaking his head.

"He's just not as into football as you are," I said.

"But he acts like he's so much better than everyone else." Harrison pounded the back of his seat. "And he thinks it's a felony if you make a joke about his stupid hat!"

It was weird to hear that Harrison thought Micah was stuck up. I guess he did sort of give that impression. "I think it's really important to him. He cares about his religion," I explained. "He probably doesn't think it's something to laugh at."

"Then he needs to get a life and stop taking himself so seriously."

I didn't have an answer for that. We drove in silence for a while, the cool air rushing over us and making my hair flap in my face, until Harrison switched on the radio. He changed the station a couple of times, then turned it off again.

"It's just like my dad says. Life is about two things: preparation and opportunity. That's exactly what happened tonight," he said. "All the time I've put in over the past couple of years. All the hours my dad and I practiced on the weekends. He was right!" Harrison shook his head like he couldn't believe it.

Austin's eyes glanced over at Harrison. I could see them in the rearview mirror, his eyebrows pinched together.

"Tonight was opportunity: a recruiter from MSU, and I rocked. I don't see what more I could do." Harrison mumbled, like he was talking to himself. "My dad was pumped."

Austin chewed his bottom lip. I had never seen that much tension on his face, not even when I told him about Eric and Wyatt's plan.

"Maybe you'd better wait and see." Austin sounded casual, but from the way he kept looking at Harrison, I could tell he didn't feel that way at all.

Harrison tapped his fist to his chest. "I have a good feeling about this."

Austin pulled into Hayden's driveway but didn't turn the car off.

"You killed tonight, but you can never tell. He might only be looking for offensive linemen." Austin spoke slowly, like each word had three meanings. Maybe he was hoping Harrison would figure out the truth.

Harrison stood up and jumped out of the car. "Don't be a buzz kill. I want to celebrate." He went off into the house without us.

Austin didn't get out of the car, so I didn't either. He tapped his fingers on the dashboard. I dug in my purse and pulled out a pack of gum. "Want some?" I asked.

He shook his head. "This wasn't a good idea. Do you mind if I bring you home?"

He wanted to take me home? My whole body sagged.

"No problem." I forced myself to smile at him, though my lips felt tight and my eyes blurred.

Austin put on some angry-sounding hard rock, and backed out of the driveway. We drove the whole way to my house without talking, and with me still sitting in the backseat.

"See you Monday," he said, when he pulled into my drive-way.

Monday? But what about our movie? Was he calling it off? I didn't know how to ask.

"Sure, Monday." I climbed out of the car and watched him drive away. Even when his car turned the corner, I could hear his stereo blaring.

AFTER AUSTIN WAS GONE, I went inside and hung my coat in the closet. Nana and Papa were at the dining-room table playing Scrabble.

"You're home early," said Papa, glancing at the grandfather clock in the corner. It was only ten-thirty.

"I was tired." I walked over behind Nana and gave her a kiss on the cheek. I wanted her to run her fingers through my hair. Offer to make me a glass of chocolate milk. Put her arms around me.

She patted my hand, but didn't say anything. She was concentrating on the game, arranging and rearranging the tiles on her rack. There was an open J near a triple word score, and she wouldn't give up until she found a way to use it. Papa was reading a book; he knew he might have to wait awhile.

I sank down into the chair next to hers, and lay my cheek on the cool table. The letters on her rack were inches in front of my nose. A word jumped out at me.

"How about this?" I asked, placing her tiles on the board and letting out a sigh.

"Jilted!" Nana patted my hand. "Marvelous. Let's see, that makes 45 points."

"She's a Scrabble genius," said Papa, putting down his book and turning the board to face him. "Are you going to help me, too? Even things up a bit." He pointed at the score pad.

"Sorry, you're on your own, Papa." I yawned. "I'm going upstairs."

I took the steps two at a time. I needed the comfort of my room. I needed to talk to Sara, even though I knew what she was going to say. I picked up my cell phone and dialed.

"Hello?" In the background, I could hear music thumping and crashing noises. It sounded like Sara was at a bowling alley.

"I'm so confused," I blurted out.

"What happened?" The tone of her voice was more annoyed than sympathetic, but I wasn't going to be picky. I needed to talk. I took a deep breath and told Sara the entire story.

"What's the confusion?" she said when I finished. "He's a jerk."

I knew she was right. I just didn't want her to be right.

"What are you guys doing tomorrow night?" I asked.

"Sure, ask us when he cancels." Sara laughed. "We're going to the poetry slam. Want to come?"

"Okay," I said. "That sounds good."

Sara screamed. Maybe someone had gotten a strike. "I'll come over early and we can hang out first," she said.

"Thank you," I said. "And I'll try not to mope."

When I hung up with Sara I climbed into bed and pulled the covers up all the way over my head. Why did Sara have to be right? I had to admit, a little part of me deep inside still hoped she wasn't. When Austin kissed me, when he asked me out, I felt something. A connection. Maybe there was some other explanation. Maybe there was still a chance.

7

The next day, Sara and I spent a couple of hours settled on the couch in front of *Mean Girls*, Sara's movie choice, and a supersized stack of magazines, my contribution to the entertainment. Sara made fun of the headlines.

"'Are you ready for S-E-X? Find out on page 182.' Thank goodness *Seventeen* published this article. How would I ever figure that out if a magazine didn't tell me? Trust my instincts? How stupid!"

"Hey," I said. "I wanted to read that." Though it was probably pointless now.

Sara flipped through the pages, then stopped. She pretended to look shocked. "It's just a list of names with yes or no. Susie Perkins: you're ready. Lila Fox: no way in hell. Essie Green: definitely not. Bambi Watkins: who are you kidding? We know you're not a virgin."

"Shut up," I said, laughing. I grabbed the magazine and hit her with it. Then the doorbell rang.

"Essie," Nana called from upstairs, "would you get the door?"

"Sure," I answered, looking at the clock. Aunt Shelli and Uncle Steve were walking over to our house for dinner. (They wouldn't drive until after sundown.) Or it could be the pizza delivery guy. It turned out my uncle would eat at our house if the meal was dairy and we ate on paper plates. Papa had made a big deal out of that. I guessed Uncle Steve used to be a lot more strict. I even overheard Papa tell Nana that if Steve had been willing to compromise ten years ago, all our lives would have been different. I knew he couldn't mean that the split between them started because Uncle Steve wouldn't eat at our house, but I had no idea what else he could mean. The doorbell rang again.

"We're coming!" Sara called. "Keep your pants on."

I laughed but covered her mouth with my hand. "Shhhh! What if they heard you?"

"Ooops. Sorry!" she shouted through my fingers to whoever was outside.

When I opened the door, Austin stood on my front porch in jeans and a snug sweater that showed off his muscles. My own muscles froze in surprise. He was the last person I expected to see standing there. I couldn't even speak.

And I was wearing a huge baggy sweatshirt.

And my hair was in a frizzy ponytail.

"Austin," Sara said, poking my back. "Hi."

"Hi," Austin answered, but it sounded more like a question than a greeting. He raised his eyebrows at me. "Do I have the wrong time? I thought we said seven."

"I thought we canceled," I said, biting my lip as my shock faded into joy. He was here. We had a date. He *did* like me.

Then Sara pinched the back of my arm. Oh. Sara. I couldn't bail on her now.

"Canceled?" Austin laughed. "Why would you think that?"

"Because of yesterday." Why had I listened to my paranoia? I wished I could split myself in half so that I could be with both of them. "You said, 'See you Monday.' "

"I did?" Austin scratched his head like he couldn't remember. "I was in a funny mood. Why didn't you say something?"

Why didn't I?

"You seemed like you wanted to be alone. I was just trying to . . ." I paused. This was too awkward. The two people I most wanted to be with. I wished one of them would let me off the hook.

I looked over my shoulder at Sara. She narrowed her eyes.

I turned back to Austin. "Uh, this is my friend Sara."

"Hey," he said.

"Hi, again," Sara said, crossing her arms over her chest.

Austin scuffed the bottom of his shoe against my doorframe. "So, I guess I should . . . um . . ."

I didn't want him to leave. I wanted to kiss him again, but Sara was standing right there. "Okay, so . . ." I couldn't finish my thought either.

"Actually, I could go to the poetry slam early. Skye might want some moral support," Sara said.

Now I felt even worse. Sara thought I wanted her to leave so that I could be alone with Austin. And it was true. I was the worst friend ever!

I looked back and forth between the two of them.

"We could all hang out together. Have you ever been to a poetry slam?" I asked Austin.

He shook his head no.

"Then you have to come," I said. "Everyone should go to a poetry slam once in their lives. And Skye's really good."

Austin squinted at Sara. She shrugged.

"Okay," he said, but he didn't sound too thrilled. Austin came inside and Sara stepped behind him to close the door. You owe me, she mouthed. Then she walked ahead of us back to the family room.

I went into the kitchen to get them both Cokes, keeping one eye on the doorway so I could see what was happening between them. I tried to convince myself that this night wasn't going to be a total disaster.

Austin stared at Sara and at her jeans, which were covered with drawings, and at her Mickey Mouse T-shirt with an inked-in mustache and buckteeth. She stared back at Austin.

"Have you known Essie a long time?" he asked.

"Since birth." Sara pulled the cap off her Sharpie and started another picture by her right knee. "We used to be next-door neighbors."

"I can't imagine growing up without my parents." Austin stared at Sara's leg. I poured the Coke too high. Fizz bubbled all over the counter. I grabbed a paper towel and watched Sara stare down Austin like she wanted to pinch him, hard.

"You know, Essie's been through a lot," she said, pointing her marker at him. "And she has people looking out for her."

Austin shifted backward in his seat. I think he thought Sara was going to pinch him, too. Or ink a mustache on his face.

"I've never met anyone like her," Austin said. "She's *real*. And sweet. You know what I mean?"

Sara nodded. She put the finishing touches on her latest drawing. "Look. I drew your portrait."

Austin laughed. "I don't think my head's that big."

Sara laughed, too. "We'll see," she said, and I hurried back with the drinks, while things between them were still relatively friendly.

"Who was at the door?" Nana asked, walking into the room. "Oh, hello," she said when she saw Austin.

"Nana, this is Austin," I said. "Austin, this is my grandmother."

"Hi, Mrs. Green," Austin said. "That's a beautiful sweater."

"Thank you, dear." Nana smiled at him. "You know, I think I'll call Shelli and tell her to bring Micah. Then you can be a foursome."

When Nana left to make the call, Sara raised her eyebrows at me. "Micah? This night keeps getting more and more interesting."

"Micah from football?" Austin looked at me, confused. "How do your grandparents know *him*?"

The words sat in my mouth. *He's my cousin.* Why couldn't I say them? "They've just known his parents forever."

Sara kicked my foot; I couldn't look at her. It wasn't exactly a lie. What I'd said was true. Besides, our families had acted as if we weren't related for almost my entire life. What was another day or two? I'd tell Austin eventually. Once I knew how he really felt about me.

I WAS UPSTAIRS changing and defrizzing my hair when I heard the doorbell ring again. I quickly stepped into my shoes and raced downstairs so that Micah and I ended up coming into the family room at the same time.

"Austin, hi," he said. "I didn't expect to see you here."

"Ditto," Austin answered.

Micah sat down in the armchair, and I went to the couch. "No one told me you had friends over," he said to me. "I didn't mean to interrupt."

"You're not interrupting!" What else could I say? Now I had even more guilt. "Micah, this is Sara Lewis." I hoped he wouldn't say anything about being related to me.

"Hi," said Sara, giving him the kind of look she always made fun of when she saw other girls doing it. I'm sure she'd claim she never looked at guys with anything other than kick-butt female power. "I think I have AP bio right after you. Sometimes I see you leaving the room."

"You're the girl who writes 'Worse Than Death.'" Micah pulled out his wallet and held up a comic strip he'd cut out from this year's first issue of the *Pershing Reporter*. "This was hysterical."

"I've never seen anyone do that with my strip before," Sara said, and she actually blushed. I couldn't remember the last time I'd seen her blush.

"Oh," said Austin. "I didn't realize that was you. I read your strip every week, too."

Sara thanked Austin, but I could tell she just wanted to know more about what Micah thought.

The doorbell rang. This time it had to be the pizza. I jumped up and asked Austin if he'd help me carry it in. I had no idea how we'd make it through dinner without someone revealing the fact that Micah was my cousin, but then Nana suggested that we eat in the kitchen while the adults ate in the dining room. I was so relieved that I didn't even care when she poured us all glasses of milk and added bendy straws. There might be a chance of getting out of the house without Austin learning the truth. After dinner, I suggested that we skip dessert and go right to the poetry slam.

THE SCHOOL CAFETERIA was decorated to look like a hip coffee shop. The regular tables were stacked against the wall, and there were about a dozen small bistro sets covered with paisley tablecloths and candles. I counted about twenty people. Zoe and Skye sat right in front of the microphone stand, but two guys from the newspaper were sitting with them, so Sara and I grabbed seats at the back of the room, and Austin and Micah went to the refreshment table.

Mr. Farrell, the English teacher running the slam, stood up on the stage and thanked everyone for coming. Sara whispered to me behind her hand, "So you and Micah are just family friends?"

"It's complicated."

"What's complicated? You're cousins. End of story."

How could I explain it to her without sounding completely shallow? All right, so maybe it was a little shallow, but it wasn't as if Micah was telling everyone we were cousins, either.

Micah placed two overflowing plates of cookies in front of us, and Austin carefully set down the four cups of coffee he'd been carrying. A black-haired girl from the junior varsity cheerleading squad stared at our table, at Austin, as though she couldn't believe he was here.

"All right, everyone, this poetry slam isn't a competition, but there are still rules," Mr. Farrell announced. "You can read something you wrote yourself, or you can recite someone else's poem. There are photocopied packets of poems at the back of the room if you didn't come prepared. Only one turn per person until everyone who wants to has gone, then you can go again. I'm not going to call on people, so just pop up when you're ready. You don't have to recite, but consider giving it a try. You might surprise yourself."

"I didn't even know our school had a poetry slam," Austin said to me.

Of course he didn't. No one in his crowd ever went to something as geeky as this, no matter how fun it was. I wanted to disappear.

"I'm going to start us off with one of my favorite poems, 'This Be the Verse,' by Philip Larkin," Mr. Farrell said. "Oh, and I'm going to recite an edited version. If you want the real one, you'll have to look it up on the Internet . . . or better yet, buy the book."

The poem was all about how parents mess their kids up, just like they were messed up by their parents when they were kids. It ends with the poet telling everyone not to have kids of their own. It was weird for me to think about. My problems came from not having parents. I never realized I'd probably have an entirely different set of problems if my parents were still alive.

Austin held the cookie plate in front of me, and I took an oatmeal raisin. "My parents definitely screwed me up," he whispered.

"Really?" Austin was the most perfect person I knew.

"They think Travis, my older brother, walks on water. All my life they've expected me to be exactly like him, same activities, same kind of friends. I guess I used to want that, too, but lately . . ." Austin's words trailed off as Mr. Farrell tried to get the night started.

"Okay, who's next?" He stepped away from the mike stand. "Have at it."

Zoe pushed Skye out of her seat. She dragged herself to the microphone and took a deep breath. "The only way I can do this," she told everyone, "is if I close my eyes."

Skye shut her eyes and began to recite her poem from memory. It was about being blue, all the different shades of blue, and what that meant. Not just sad, like I've got the blues, but blazing electric blue feelings, and pure azure blue sky feelings, too. Her voice wavered a little as she said the last lines.

> *The Inuit know*
> *One hundred words for snow. Blue*
> *Has that many, too.*
>
> *I'll use them all, and*
> *Then I'll become colors they*
> *Haven't even invented.*

Skye opened her eyes and took in the room like she'd forgotten we were there. She blinked at us, confused for a moment, then smiled. Mr. Farrell had fixed the stage with footlights, and the way Skye's face was lit from below made her glow. She was so . . . on her way. Not just on her way to being a writer, but to being who she'd become. Her future self. Adult self. She had a path in front of her that she could see. I was standing at the beginning of my life blindfolded and someone was spinning me around, so that even when I could eventually see again, I'd still have no idea which way to go.

Austin took a bite out of his chocolate chip cookie, then said with his mouth full, " 'S good." It came out a little too loud, and I shushed him, but then I noticed Mr. Farrell nod and smile in our direction. I think he thought Austin was talking about Skye's poem. Maybe he *was* talking about the poem. Everyone in the room was clapping.

There was another lull and Mr. Farrell shouted from his seat, "Come on. I know it's a hard act to follow, but be brave."

A freshman boy with puffy hair stood up next and read a funny poem about his best friend—his goldfish. When he finished, Sara brought us a couple of the poetry packets.

"We should do it," she said. Micah took one and Sara slid the other across the table to Austin and me. Then she scooted closer to Micah so they could share.

Austin picked up the packet and started flipping through it. I studied his face, trying to figure out what he was thinking. Maybe he was worried that going out with me would mean poetry slams 24/7. Maybe he was reconsidering our date. Maybe . . .

Austin tilted his head next to mine. I could feel his breath on my ear. Was he going to tell me how much this night sucked?

"I think I should tell Harrison the truth," he whispered. "That there was no recruiter."

Oh. So different from what I'd been thinking. And his voice sounded more than just concerned. It sounded scared.

"Why?" I asked.

"He and his dad are obsessed. They're making all these phone calls, trying to figure out who the scout was. His dad really sees this as Harrison's chance."

"Yeah, but after they can't find anything out, they'll drop it," I whispered. "Right?"

Austin shook his head. His eyebrows knotted.

"I just don't want to put Harrison through all that. You have no idea how intense his dad can be. It got even worse two years ago, after his mom and sister moved to Atlanta. The only thing his dad thinks about is where Harrison will play football. I'm afraid his dad is going to flip out and it'll be my fault."

"It won't be your fault," I said, but I knew what he meant. "Maybe his dad will surprise you."

Austin leaned back, ran his fingers through his hair, and then stared at the ceiling. I wished I could do something to make him feel better.

I stood up.

"What are you doing?" Austin asked, grabbing my hand.

"Cheering you up," I said. I went to the microphone and recited "Warning," a Shel Silverstein poem I memorized in fourth grade for a school project and still remembered. It was about a snail that lives in your nostril and will bite your finger off if you pick your nose.

When I finished, Austin hooted like he was at a rock concert. I laughed, and Mr. Farrell said, "That's the spirit."

"Okay, you convinced me," Austin said when I returned to the table. He took the poetry packet up to the microphone.

"This poem is called 'Football,' by Louis Jenkins," he said. It was about a football player who suddenly realizes he's holding a shoe instead of the ball. About how sometimes you have to make compromises, and sometimes you can't compromise. He read it really well.

Later in the evening, Sara and Micah read a poem together called "Did I Miss Anything?" and Austin held my hand. For a moment I had a flash of him becoming part of my world instead of the other way around. As if that could ever happen.

BACK AT MY HOUSE, Micah walked Sara to her car and I stayed in the Jeep for another moment with Austin. He'd been quiet on the ride home, and now he gripped the steering wheel so hard his knuckles turned white.

"Tonight was fun," he said, though his voice didn't really sound like he meant it.

"Do you want to come over for dinner one night this week?" I asked. Over for dinner? I probably sounded ten years old. I might as well tell him Nana was making Kraft Mac & Cheese with cut-up hot dogs.

Austin kept looking straight ahead. He didn't answer for a second. His silence made me curse myself. He'd shown up for our date, and instead of a date, I dragged him out with Sara and Micah to a school function. Now I was acting like we were in fifth grade.

I was about to get out of the car without saying goodbye when Austin exhaled deeply and squeezed my hand. "How about Tuesday? After practice."

I nodded. Austin put his hand on the back of my neck and drew me close for a kiss. His cologne made my thoughts spin, and our second kiss lasted so much longer than the first one. Every time the kissing softened and slowed, I thought Austin would pull away. But he kept going, his hand sliding down to my shoulder, then to my upper arm, than tracing my collarbone. Where was it headed?

I pulled back.

"What's the matter?" Austin asked.

"I thought I heard my grandmother calling," I lied.

Austin looked over my shoulder at my front door, shut tight. "Nope," he said. "Must have been your imagination."

"I guess so."

Could I have acted any more inexperienced? I wished I could have a do-over. But Austin had already shifted back into the driver's seat. His hands were on the wheel.

"See you at school," he said.

"Yeah, school." I climbed out of the car, watched Austin drive away, then headed to my house.

Before I even put my hand on the doorknob, I could hear shouting. Nana and Papa? I'd never heard them fight like that before. I flung the door open. Other voices were yelling, too. My aunt and uncle.

"You don't get to decide how I raise Micah," my uncle shouted, "so stay out of it! Do I criticize the fact that you brought Essie up without any sense of her people or her culture? Let alone without any spirituality?"

"Oh, Steve, don't go there. Your father didn't mean anything by his comment," Aunt Shelli said. "You're overreacting. Everyone in this room agrees that Micah should be able to make his own choices. Including you."

Micah was sitting on the stairs in the foyer. Everyone else was in the living room. I sat next to him. The shouting fizzled down to strained conversation. I couldn't hear what they were saying anymore, and I didn't want to know. Suddenly it seemed obvious why we had gone so many years without visits. Micah took the clip off his kippah and clicked it back and forth in his hands.

"Do you and your dad fight over religion a lot?" I asked.

Micah shook his head. "Never. Not until this football thing."

"Doesn't it bother you that you have to follow so many arbitrary rules?"

"I don't have to follow them. I want to follow them. They don't feel arbitrary to me. You wouldn't know it from the way he's been acting since we moved back here, but my dad is really open to me making my own choices. I think being around Papa just makes him really defensive."

"But Papa's trying really hard not to offend your dad."

"I know. They're just too similar, so they're really good at pushing each other's buttons."

"Similar! They're exact opposites."

"Not really. After your parents died . . ." Micah stopped. I thought he might be wondering if I'd be okay with talking about my parents so I nodded at him. "After your parents died," Micah continued, "Papa and my dad had completely opposite reactions. Before, they'd both been on the same page, religiously speaking, meaning they both were a little bit observant, but not that much. But after, Papa turned away from Judaism completely and my dad let it take over his life. He used to be consumed by it. Spending all his free time studying, really blocking out the world. I think he was looking for answers."

"You remember all this?"

"Some, and my mom told me the rest."

I tried to imagine Nana telling me even *half* of what Micah'd just said, but I couldn't. It seemed so unfair that he got to know everything while I knew nothing. It seemed more mine to know. After all, it was *my* parents who'd died. "So that's the reason they wouldn't talk. That's why we went so many years without seeing each other?"

"Well, there was more to it than that." Micah glanced at the doorway to the living room. "Now isn't the right time to talk about it, though."

"Oh." I could see that he was right, but I didn't want to wait. And this was the second time Micah was holding back. "Does this have anything to do with the thing you wouldn't tell me last week?"

Micah's eyes flitted toward the living room again. "I really don't think we should talk about it here," he said.

"Fine," I answered. It was clear he wasn't going to change his mind, but I wasn't happy about it. I ran my hand over the carpet on the stairs. If he wasn't going to tell me the truth about our family, what else was there to talk about?

"How come you never told the guys on the team the reason why you walk home?" I asked.

"Would it have made any difference?" Micah shrugged.

I looked at the ceiling. "It might make things better. When people don't know the reasons for things, they have to make up their own explanations."

"You mean like when people don't know that we're cousins, so they think that I like you?" Micah stared at me. His eyes weren't angry or sad; they were just matter-of-fact. That was almost worse.

A bubble of guilt rose in my throat and stuck midway.

"You mean Lara?"

"Lara and some guys on the team."

I bit my lip. "Have you told them?"

He shook his head. "Like I've said, they don't really talk *to* me, only about me. Besides, I had this feeling that maybe that information was yours to share."

I didn't know what to say. After a few seconds of silence, Micah turned back to his kippah clip and didn't look at me anymore. I should have been trying to make him feel welcome at Pershing, but instead I'd been pretending we weren't related. I tried to think of an apology, but Aunt Shelli and Uncle Steve walked in.

"Time to go," Uncle Steve said. "Nana's going to give us a ride home."

Micah and I stood, and Aunt Shelli kissed me goodbye. I hugged Uncle Steve, then Micah and I looked at each other.

"Night," he finally said.

"Good night," I answered, not understanding where things stood between us now. Or where I wanted them to stand.

8

The football team had practice until six every day after school, and then Austin had to shower and give Harrison a ride home. He told me he might not make it over for dinner until close to seven. Normally Nana hated to eat late, but she and Papa had a ballroom dancing class, so they were going to pick up Chinese food on the way home.

On Tuesday evening, when Austin rang my doorbell at six-twenty, I nearly fainted. He must have raced over. Nana and Papa were out, and I wasn't sure what they'd say when they got home and found Austin already here.

When I told Austin my grandparents were gone, he looked at me sideways.

"What are you suggesting?" he asked.

"Uh . . ." I couldn't think of a reply. Had I been suggesting something? All day I had been imagining us on the couch after dinner, watching *Titanic*. Nana and Papa would be in the dining room working on a puzzle. I'd turn the lights low and make popcorn. When Rose and Jack meet, Austin would put his arm around my shoulder, and we'd snuggle. We couldn't do anything more than that with my grandparents in the next room.

"Want to watch a movie?" I asked.

Austin glanced up the stairs. My bedroom door was open at the top of the staircase.

"Oh. Uh, do you want to see my room?" Suddenly I felt almost too weak to stand. I couldn't tell if I was excited or panicked. I'd never shown a guy my bedroom. I hadn't even taken Austin upstairs *in my imagination*.

"Do you want to show it to me?" he answered. His eyes held mine so tightly I couldn't look away. I needed a second to think.

"How's Harrison?" I asked, trying to distract him.

"That's right, I didn't tell you!" Austin smacked his palm against his forehead. "You're not going to believe it." He turned away from the staircase and walked past me into the kitchen.

I looked upstairs and tried to imagine kissing Austin on my bed. We'd start out sitting on the edge, then we'd slowly lean back, and then . . .

"Do you have any Coke?" he called.

And then I went into the kitchen, too. "On the bottom shelf of the refrigerator," I said.

"A glass?" he asked.

I pointed to the cabinet.

Austin grabbed one and sat down at the table. "It's the weirdest coincidence."

I sat down next to him. "What?" I asked, though a part of me couldn't stop thinking about my bedroom.

"Maybe you're psychic," he said, taking a sip of Coke. "Because there *was* a recruiter at the game."

"Really?"

"The guy was from Ferris State. Division II. I'm not sure he's interested in Harrison, but somehow Harrison's dad got the guy to agree to watch another game. He's coming this Friday. Harrison's dad doesn't take no for an answer."

"So everything worked out."

Austin shrugged. "I just hope he wants Harrison. His dad started talking to schools when Harrison was fourteen; he was unbelievable then. Nobody's made an offer, though. This could be Harrison's last chance. It'll be pretty rough at his house if nothing happens."

Austin took another drink. "It's ironic. For the past two years, Harrison's dad made him throw away any mail that came from Division II schools. He was sure Harrison had Division I potential. Now it looks like Division II is his only chance. The problem is, I know how twisted his dad'll be about it. It's no-win. Harrison's a loser if all he can play is Division II ball, but he's an even bigger loser if he doesn't play anywhere."

"He's lucky to have you as a friend," I said. I could tell Austin was genuinely worried.

Austin sighed. "Sometimes it's hard work."

I nodded.

"Hey. I never told you about Wyatt and Eric," Austin said, changing the subject. "After the game, Coach overheard them in the locker room talking about ditching me next week. They're benched for three games."

"That's good, right?"

"Depends how well the second-string guys play. Eric and Wyatt weren't actually that bad. Look, I know you don't want to tell me, but I have to know. Who told you?" He took my hands and waited for my answer.

I pictured Micah's face. The way he looked when he told me he'd never be part of the team. What if he was wrong? Maybe Austin knowing the truth would change everything.

"You can't tell him I told you, promise?"

Austin held up three fingers. "Scout's honor."

It would be better if I told, I was pretty sure. Austin rubbed his thumb against the back of my hand. "I just want to return the favor," he said.

"It was Micah," I answered.

Austin nodded, but didn't say anything. We sat at the kitchen table holding hands, with me dying to know what was going on in his brain. Was he thinking of ways to thank Micah? Or was he thinking of ways to forget what he'd just heard? I couldn't ask.

"So, what do you want to do?" I finally said.

Austin hooked his leg around mine under the table. "Do you still want to show me your bedroom?"

Oh yeah. My bedroom. With its baby-yellow curtains and stuffed animal collection. Still the same as when I was a little girl. Taking Austin up there was about as far from little girl as I could get. I was about to say yes when I heard the garage door open. My grandparents were home. I breathed a sigh of relief.

"We'd better find something to do quick, or they'll recruit us to

work on their new puzzle. Three thousand pieces of wheat field,"
I said.

Austin held his arm up and tilted his head to the side in a way
that made it look like he was hanging from a noose. We went
into the family room, just as Nana and Papa came in through the
garage.

"Essie?" Nana called out. "Is Austin here?"

"We're in the family room," I called back. "Austin got here a
little early." Nana came into the room and glanced around uneas-
ily.

"Sorry, Mrs. Green," Austin apologized. "I didn't realize you'd
be out."

Nana's face was suspicious, but she offered him a drink anyway.

"No, thank you. I just had one."

"Well, okay." Nana looked unconvinced. Who knows what
she thought we were doing?

"Essie tells me you do puzzles," Austin said. "I love puzzles."

Nana's face lit up. "We have a new one. We planned to start
after dinner. Would you like to help?"

"Sure," Austin told her. If I hadn't known better, I would have
thought puzzles were his favorite thing in the world.

All through dinner Austin kept my grandparents entertained
with stories about football. Then after dinner we sat with Nana
and Papa for two hours arranging the tiny beige pieces of the wheat
field. Austin made Nana's evening, but I couldn't help noticing
how easily he could make something that wasn't true sound so
very believable.

———

"WHERE WERE YOU last night?" Sara asked as she picked me up for school the next morning. "I texted you a million times."

The corners of my mouth pulled up involuntarily as I answered, "Austin came over." I hadn't even checked my phone after he left. I spent the rest of the night daydreaming about accidentally getting locked in the equipment closet at school with Austin. "Then I had homework. Sorry."

I pulled my phone out of my backpack and flipped it open. In reality, she'd only sent four texts, but that was a lot for Sara. "What's up?"

"Nothing." Sara acted like it was no big deal, but I could see there was something she wasn't sharing.

"Spill it." It was weird; usually Sara was the one convincing *me* to talk.

She spoke softly. "Micah's a lot different than I'd imagined."

"You shouldn't judge a football player by his cover." I grinned.

"So . . ." Sara took a deep breath. She was so fidgety. "He called me yesterday. We talked for two hours."

I knew she thought he was cute, and I could see that they'd really connected at the poetry slam, but the two-hour phone call still caught me off guard. My brain went fuzzy. I should be happy for her. I could see that Sara and Micah would be really perfect together, but something inside me was screaming no. This couldn't be happening. "Are you guys going to go out?"

"It's nothing like that. We just had an amazing conversation. That's all."

"Okay," I said. *Good.*

"I like talking to him," she added, pulling into the spot right across from where Austin always parked. She must have been distracted or she never would have parked so close. Austin's car was already there. "I can't believe he carries one of my strips in his wallet."

"You just met," I said. "There's still a lot you don't know about him. He could be into professional wrestling or romance novels or . . ."

"Holy crap! There he is." Sara pulled down her visor and checked her face in the mirror as Micah got out of the passenger side of Austin's car, followed by Harrison. Austin got out on the other side.

"Come on," Sara said.

As soon as Austin saw me, he kissed me hello. In front of every person there. Then he grabbed my hand and we all started walking toward school together.

"Thanks for the lift," Micah told Austin. "I appreciate it."

"No problem." Austin wiggled his fingers against mine. "Same time tomorrow?"

"Uh," Micah glanced at Harrison. "Sure, I guess. But I'm not exactly on your way."

"More like miles out of the way," Harrison muttered.

Austin ignored him. "I don't mind. It was nice to talk about something other than . . ." Austin stopped and looked at Harrison, who was looking back at him with a mix of disbelief and anger. "Just to talk about life and the news and stuff."

Micah still didn't look too sure.

"I could pick you up if you need a ride," Sara suggested. "You're only the next subdivision over from me."

"That'd be great." Micah jumped at her offer. "It's probably better," he said to Austin. "It seems easier this way."

Austin shrugged, but I thought his feelings looked hurt. "Whatever's good for you."

"Well, thanks for today anyway," Micah said.

"The offer's still open for Friday nights," Austin added. "If you ever change your mind."

Micah nodded, even though I knew changing his mind about that wasn't going to happen. "I'll see you guys later." He waved goodbye and hurried ahead of us. Sara followed him.

"I've got to talk to Mr. Kramer before school," she called back to me.

Yeah, right, I thought.

After they were gone, Harrison cleared his throat and spit on the sidewalk. "What was that about? Be Kind to Freaks Week?" he asked.

Austin frowned. "Maybe I'd just like to hang out with someone other than the same five people for a change."

Harrison's gray eyes flashed. "Well, you're lucky the smart chick's into him. What were you going to do, drive him the whole year?"

"He's not that bad." Austin quickened his pace, and I almost tripped keeping up with him.

"Right," Harrison said. "Did you notice how fast he tried to get away?"

Austin shrugged. "Whatever. I'm not driving him anyway, so drop it."

"What is wrong with you this year?" Harrison asked. "You're almost as bad as he is."

As soon as we got to the courtyard, Harrison stormed off without saying goodbye. Hayden and Lara were sitting on the first bench. Harrison went right to them and kissed Lara before sitting down next to her. She leaned into him and crossed both legs over his lap.

Lara and Harrison?

"Sorry about that," Austin said.

I wasn't exactly sure what he was apologizing for. What happened with Micah? Fighting with Harrison? "Don't worry about it," I said.

Austin stared at Harrison. "I wish it was that easy."

9

Pershing's turnout on Friday night was really big for an away game. Farmington Hills was only twenty minutes from Pershing. Ms. Young didn't even get a bus for the cheerleaders. We carpooled.

Coach Ryan had been plugging the game all week during morning announcements, telling the school that we were going to have the best season we'd had since *he'd* played for Pershing. As the cheerleaders took the field, my ears rang from the screams. When the football team ran out, I couldn't stop thinking about Harrison and the scout. This was his chance. Somewhere in the stands was a coach from Ferris State. Tonight could change Harrison's life.

After the huddle, I saw Harrison scanning the crowd. Then his father, wearing a dark suit and a tie, walked over to him. He put his hands on Harrison's shoulders and spoke, his mouth twisting, never once letting his eyes leave Harrison's. When he was finished, Harrison nodded and punched a fist into the palm of his other hand.

Pershing won the coin toss and luck seemed to be on our side.

Harrison scored his first touchdown within five minutes. At the end of the first half, we were up 14 to 3. Harrison was on fire. Austin kept setting him up and Harrison kept delivering. He wasn't letting his opportunity go to waste.

During halftime it started to drizzle. The crowd in the stands thinned out; people went for hot dogs, then didn't come back. The rain made everything slippery, and the rest of the cheerleaders and I felt damp and miserable. Ms. Young wouldn't let us stunt in this kind of weather, so basically all we could do was step side to side and clap. Lara kept complaining that there wasn't any point to the cheerleaders being at the game if we couldn't do our stunts.

The players ran back out onto the field for the third quarter, but the momentum had changed. Our defense couldn't hold Farmington, and by the end of the third quarter the game was tied. Nothing much happened in the fourth quarter. Each team held the other scoreless, but with less than a minute to go, Harrison caught one at the five-yard line and stepped out of bounds to stop the clock with two seconds left. All Micah had to do was kick an easy field goal. The players on the bench were already giving each other high fives.

Micah lined up for the kick. He ran forward, the defense rushing at him, but he slipped on the wet grass, and the kick went wide right. Everyone groaned. We were going into overtime.

We stopped Farmington on their possession and took over at the ten-yard line. If we scored, we would win. I bit my lip; I couldn't take my eyes from the game. Austin took the snap but didn't have much time to get his pass off. Harrison was open, and Austin lobbed it. The throw was high. Harrison had to jump. He came down with it, but as he landed something went wrong. His right knee bent at a funny angle. I cringed before he was fully on the ground.

The way he writhed and clutched at his leg made my own knee ache. Half the people in the stands moaned. The other half of the crowd erupted into cheers. Harrison was in the end zone. We'd won. The cheering went on a few seconds more, then the sounds from the bleachers began to taper off. The lights shined down on Harrison's body.

The players just stood around, but not too close to Harrison, still lying on the ground. Only Austin kneeled by his side.

When the trainer arrived on the field, Harrison couldn't stand. He had to be carried off on a stretcher. I wondered where his father was now. Not on the field. Nana and Papa would have been the first ones by my side if it had been me. As he was carried past the sidelines, Harrison stared out into the night.

AFTER THE GAME Hayden drove me back to Pershing and I waited by Austin's car with Lara, Hayden, and a couple of other cheerleaders for news about Harrison. Mist hung in the air and made my skin clammy and cold.

"It could be really bad," Lara said. "If he tore his ACL, he'll need surgery."

"It might only be a sprain," said Hayden. Lara pressed her fingers to her lips, and Hayden put an arm around her shoulder.

"You know what?" Lara looked at me like she was about to say something really important. A shiver twisted my shoulders, and I stuffed my hands into my pockets. "None of this would have happened if that loser Geekberg hadn't missed the field goal."

"I know, right?" Hayden said.

I knew Lara wanted to be angry at somebody, but it wasn't fair to blame Micah. What about Austin? He'd thrown the bad pass. The truth was that injury was part of the game sometimes. It wasn't anyone's fault.

"It *was* raining," I said, but before I could say another word, Lara shot me a look so cold a shudder ran up my back.

"What's going on between the two of you, anyway?" she asked. "Because your feelings for him are clouding your judgment."

"Nothing is going on between us." Everyone stared at me.

This was all my fault. I should have told everyone he was my cousin to begin with. Maybe they wouldn't have treated him any differently, but at least I wouldn't have had to hear them talk like this about him. I looked down at the pavement in the parking lot, still slick and shiny damp from the rain. It seemed too late to tell the truth now. I'd look like an idiot.

"There they are," Lara said as Austin and a couple of guys from the team walked out of school.

"He's at Mount Sinai Hospital," Austin told us. "They sent him for an MRI." His voice sounded drained of emotion. He took my hand. "I'm going to head over there now."

I tried to focus on his words, but he was playing with my fingers as he spoke. I wished he would stay with me instead of going to the hospital.

"Can you get a ride home?" he asked.

I looked at Hayden.

"No problem," she said.

Just before we all went our separate ways, Austin kissed me on the cheek and whispered in my ear, "This is all my fault." Even with his hand so warm in mine, goose bumps ran up my arm.

AUSTIN PICKED ME UP at seven the next night and we went out to dinner. I hadn't heard from him all day, so the first thing I asked when I got in the car was "How's Harrison?"

"He tore his ACL. He's going to need surgery. They just have to wait for the swelling to go down. He won't talk to anyone. Not even me."

"What will happen with Ferris State?" I asked.

"Well, they're not going to recruit him this year. Maybe he'll be able to walk on somewhere next year, but it's kind of a long shot." Austin let out a sigh and pulled into the parking lot of Amir's. "Depends how well he recuperates. I'm sure his dad will have him working his butt off."

"Is his dad . . ." I didn't even know how to finish that sentence. Upset? Taking care of him? Acting crazy?

"You don't want to know."

After we'd been seated and the waitress had taken our order, I tried to get Austin's mind off things by telling him stories about my geometry teacher, Mr. Oblonsky; his strangeness was Pershing legend. Mr. Oblonsky was the kind of teacher who sometimes forgot that his students were in the room with him. When he got really absorbed in a problem, he talked or sang to himself.

"Oh!" I said, as the waitress set our food on the table. "I thought of another one. Okay, this is bad. Once I tell you, you might not be able to eat."

"I'm tough," Austin said.

"Yesterday, during a pop quiz, Mr. Oblonsky blew his nose and left a huge glob of mucus on the tip of it for the rest of the period."

Austin cringed. "That's pretty bad. Sean told me he once saw him eating a little green guy."

"Disgusting," I said, laughing. Austin reached over and stole a fry off my plate. I tapped the back of his hand. "Hey!" He smiled his slow smile, the one I dreamed about every night.

"Here." Austin held the fry up to my mouth. "You want it back?"

I took a bite, then he ate the other half. "Thanks for that," he said.

"For what?"

"For making me smile," he answered. "I know I'm not such great company tonight. It's just . . . I've always felt sort of responsible for Harrison. I used to wish *he* was my brother, instead of my real brother. This is going to sound conceited, but Harrison has always looked up to me. He was the one person in my life who didn't make me feel second-best. I can't believe I did this to him."

I squeezed his leg with my ankles. "It's not your fault," I said. "It wasn't anyone's fault."

Austin shrugged. "I don't know if I'm up for a movie. Is that okay?"

"Let's skip the movie and hang out in your car instead." I'd been thinking of sitting in his car and talking, listening to music. But with the words out of my mouth, I realized what it sounded like. My breath caught in my throat as I imagined kissing him in the backseat.

Austin grabbed my hand and laced his fingers through mine. "That sounds like exactly what I need."

I tried to imagine what else Austin and I would do in his car. Suddenly my curfew seemed a long way off.

WE PARKED THE CAR in an empty lot behind an office building. Austin let the engine idle and put his iPod on a playlist called "Saturday Night." I folded my hands in my lap. Now that we were about to do whatever we were going to do in his car, I felt silly and embarrassed.

"Do you want to take off your coat?" Austin asked.

"Oh," I said. "Yeah." I tried to wiggle out of it, but couldn't get it off. Then I realized I needed to unbuckle my seat belt first. When I finally threw my jacket in the backseat, Austin was laughing at me.

"It's not that funny," I said, but I laughed, too. Then Austin kissed me. He still tasted like French fries. I buried my hands in his hair.

Austin reached around me and pushed the seat's recline handle. The back gave way with a bump, and suddenly he was lying in my seat with me, half on top of me. I snuggled into him, kissed him again, and sighed happily. The kisses felt so good I wanted them to last all night.

Then his hand brushed my stomach and the button on my jeans. I wasn't lost in kisses anymore. The only thing I could focus on was my button. And what would happen if it opened. We kept kissing, and Austin moved his hand to my shoulder, but I knew that it was only a matter of time until it found my jeans again. We had two hours before I needed to go home. I sat up.

"What's wrong?" Austin asked, propping himself up on his elbow.

I turned onto my side. "This feels weird."

"What does?" His eyes looked confused and sad.

My cheeks grew hot. I hadn't meant to hurt his feelings. I shook my head.

"Essie." Austin sat all the way up now. The expression on his face was so serious. "I don't know what you mean."

"We're going too fast." I blinked to hold my tears back. I didn't want to look more immature than I already did.

Austin put his arms around me and hugged me to his chest. I could feel his heart beating against my shoulder. "It's okay," he said. "There's no rush. I'll take it slower. We don't have to do anything tonight."

I nodded, my forehead nestled into the crook of his neck, and tried to swallow the lump in my throat.

Austin kissed the top of my head. "I don't know how this is going to sound . . ." He paused. "But you're the first girl who's ever asked me to wait."

A picture of a giant bed with hundreds of girls in it flashed in my mind. How many girls had he been with? And what about Vi? Hadn't she asked him to wait? How long would it be before he got sick of waiting and went to find a girl who wouldn't ask him to?

"I'm sorry," I said.

"Don't apologize. I'm saying it's a good thing. I think I like girls who ask me to wait more." Austin tilted my chin and kissed me softly. "A lot more."

But what if I never felt ready? What if Austin had to wait forever?

He moved back into the driver's seat. "So what do you want to do now?"

I shrugged. "Talk?"

He laughed. "Okay, about what?"

"I don't know. You ask me questions."

I readjusted my seat to its upright position and for a moment was sorry that I'd stopped Austin from doing whatever he'd been about to do. After lying so close, he now seemed a million miles away. He put his hands behind his head and stared at the ceiling of the car. "What's your favorite color?"

I twisted sideways so I could watch him while we talked. "Pink."

He grinned. "Do you want to be a ballerina when you grow up?"

"No." I fake-frowned at him. "Ask me serious questions."

"What do you think the stock market is going to do next week?"

"Austin!" I shoved him in the ribs. "Come on!"

"Okay, okay." He rolled over onto his side to face me. "When's your birthday?"

"I'll be sixteen on March 13th."

"All right. In the spring you'll be able to drive me around." Austin made Groucho Marx eyebrows.

I thought about the blue form still sitting in my backpack. I knew I'd never give it to Nana. "I'm not going to get my license," I said.

"Come on. You can't be that bad."

I shook my head. "I mean, I'm choosing not to get my license. And I probably am that bad a driver. I've never driven before."

Austin sat up and put his hand on the steering wheel. "Are you serious? *Never?*"

I nodded.

"You've never taken driver's ed? Never went driving with your grandparents?"

I shook my head again.

"Come on," he said, opening his door and climbing out of the car.

"Where are you going?" I called. He walked around the car to my side. My stomach dropped onto the floor mats.

"Switch seats with me," he said, opening the door. "It's time for your first driving lesson."

"I'm not allowed to drive with you. I don't have a permit. Even if I had a permit, I'd only be allowed to drive with adults. This is so illegal." I could picture Nana picking me up at the police station. The expression on her face. She'd never talk to me again.

"We're in a deserted parking lot. Nobody's going to know. You can go one mile an hour if you want to. Come on." Austin took my hand and helped me out of the car. "Isn't it kind of cool that your first time will be with me?" He winked, and my stomach jumped up into my chest. I let him walk me around to the driver's side and I climbed in. I knew it was wrong, that Nana would die if she knew, but I couldn't say no.

10

After that night, Austin called me every day. Maybe it was because he felt so comfortable confiding his worries about Harrison to me. Or maybe it was because of the secret driving lesson. But we talked about much more than that. How his parents wanted him to go to U of M, like his older brother. His brother had just pledged Sigma Alpha Epsilon; Austin's dad had been in that fraternity, too. Austin would be a legacy. I told Austin about dance, how some years I took five classes a week, and even now could wake up on Saturday morning and put my leotard on before I remembered that I didn't take dance lessons anymore. Sometimes we didn't even talk. We'd just leave our cell phones on speaker while we did our homework together, making random comments every now and then.

At school, Austin waited by his car until I arrived each morning and held my hand whenever we were together. Tuesday afternoon he stopped by cheerleading practice before we started to give me a quick kiss hello. Lara commented on it as soon as he left. "You guys are so cute together it's sickening," she said.

"You should eat lunch with us tomorrow," Hayden said.

On Wednesday, I found Zoe and Skye in the hallway and told them I wouldn't be at our table in the cafeteria.

"Why not?" Zoe asked, smiling. "Don't want to be seen with us anymore?"

"No!" I said, even though I knew she was teasing. "I love eating with you guys. It's just that Hayden asked."

She bumped me with her hip. "Oh, right. Wouldn't want to say no to Hayden."

"It's not that," I stammered.

"Leave her alone," Skye said to Zoe. "It's fine," she told me. "We still love you no matter who you eat with."

I didn't know which was worse, Zoe's teasing or Skye's loyalty. "Do you . . . um, do you want to all eat together?"

Zoe burst out laughing. "No thanks," she said, shooing me away from her. "Go. Go eat with the pretty people. We'll see you later."

Even Skye shook her head. "You can eat with us tomorrow," she said.

WEDNESDAY WAS HARRISON'S first day back since his injury. He was on crutches, and his knee was in a brace. At lunch it took some maneuvering to get us all settled into the booth. Harrison sat on the end with his leg propped up on a chair, and Lara sat on his other side, so close she was practically in his lap.

Everyone had a million questions about his surgery. He answered all of them like he was giving a press conference. We learned that he wasn't taking the pain meds because he wanted his mind and body to be sharp. He was already starting physical therapy—four days a week, way more than insurance would pay for. He planned on being in top shape by the summer.

Austin didn't say anything.

Across the cafeteria, Micah sat at a table with two guys. One of them wore a bright green T-shirt that read "Mmmmm . . . π." He said something and made a face. Micah and the other guy burst out laughing.

"Are you going to go to practices anymore?" Hayden asked him.

"I'm still on the team," Harrison said.

Hayden nodded. "What will you do, just watch?"

Harrison's jaw bulged, and he worked visibly to relax. "I have a new role on the team. I'm going to help coach the receivers. Especially my replacement."

"You mean Micah?" I asked, glancing at his table.

Poisonous looks came at me from all directions, but no one answered. Finally Harrison muttered, "Yeah. I mean Gruenberg."

"Can you believe it?" Lara said. "He flubs the kick and then gets moved up. He's probably thrilled."

Even though at the beginning of the season Micah had been upset that he'd never get a chance to play receiver, I doubted he was happy about the way everything was working out. But I didn't say so.

"It was my fault," Austin said. "My pathetic throw." He sounded like he'd lost his best friend. I rubbed his shoulder.

"It wasn't your fault," Harrison protested. "We shouldn't have been on the field. The game should have been over. Gruenberg makes the kick, we win, my knee is fine."

It was completely faulty logic, but who could argue with a guy whose future in football had just disappeared? He needed someone to blame. No one was going to tell him no. I followed Harrison's eyes across the cafeteria. They'd locked onto Micah.

Micah, who should have made the kick. Micah, who was the new wide receiver.

I watched Sara sit down next to Micah. She picked up his apple and took a bite. He pretended to be upset, but his eyes told the truth. He liked her. Something was definitely going to happen between them. And then he'd be the boyfriend of my best friend *and* the enemy of my boyfriend's best friend. Was it even possible to be both of those things at the same time? What if I had to choose?

I turned to Austin. He gave me a super-slow smile that made me stop worrying. I was his girlfriend. That was all. I slid my hand across the bench of the booth, hooked my pinky finger to his under the table, and reminded myself that I couldn't have done that if I was sitting across the cafeteria with Sara and Micah.

WITHOUT HARRISON the Panthers weren't at the top of their game. Harrison was one of a couple of guys who played both an offensive and defensive position. It took two players to replace him, two athletes starting at positions they'd only ever played in practice. Pershing lost its next two games. Micah and the new middle linebacker were playing okay, but we were up against two of the best schools in our league and our new team hadn't found its rhythm yet.

Then it was October and the Jewish High Holidays. Micah would be missing practice, on Monday, Tuesday, and Wednesday. I hadn't realized he'd be out for so many days. Monday afternoon I overheard Lara and some other cheerleaders gossiping about it. About how Micah was given this amazing opportunity to play and he was blowing it.

I woke up dreading having to go to practice after school on Tuesday. I didn't feel like hearing everyone complain even more about Micah, but as I was on my way to the shower that morning, Nana told me I should put on a dress. She was making me miss school to go to Rosh Hashanah services with Aunt Shelli. I wanted to have a tantrum when she said it, but she looked so happy and hopeful that I couldn't complain. Then I wondered, if it was making her so happy, why wasn't *she* going?

When I asked her, her eyes got a faraway look. I didn't push it. The expression on her face meant she was remembering my parents. The day was going to be torturous enough without starting it off by making Nana cry.

Aunt Shelli picked me up at nine-thirty, and I tried to be friendly, but my resentment about going to her synagogue sat like a brick wall around me, refusing to let her in.

"Steve and Micah have been there since eight," she said. "Services break for lunch at twelve-thirty."

I nodded, stifling a yawn that must have welled up in anticipation of the boredom. Two and a half endless hours. My legs itched as I followed Aunt Shelli into the synagogue; I hated wearing pantyhose.

We had to wait in a long line of people in the lobby. They were all standing behind a pair of giant wooden doors, holding on to their tickets like they were at a play or a concert. Only the ushers weren't checking the tickets; they were just making everyone wait. The men wore dark suits, kippahs, and fringy shawls, but the women looked like they were there for a day at the races. Brightly colored dresses and suits with elaborate hats. The kind nobody ever wore anymore.

"Do you remember this?" Aunt Shelli asked in a hushed voice as she gestured at the space around us. My aunt and uncle had been members of this synagogue before they moved away. I wondered if she'd taken me here sometime before.

I took in the white marble floors, the gray stone walls, and the brass sculpture of a tree filling up the corner of the room. There was a flash of something in my memory. I shook my head at her.

"Nope," I said. "Not familiar."

A woman who looked like a fancier version of Aunt Shelli came over to us.

"*Shana tovah*," she said to my aunt. At least that's what it sounded like, since I had no idea what she was saying.

"Happy New Year to you, too," Aunt Shelli replied. "Bonnie, this is my niece, Essie."

The woman turned to me, eyes wide behind the half-veil of her hat. She took my hand, "*Shana tovah*."

"Nice to meet you," I said, though she hadn't let go of my hand, and I didn't really think it was nice. I tried to loosen her grip.

"I haven't seen her since she was a little girl," the woman told Aunt Shelli, as if I wasn't even there. The woman gave my hand one last squeeze, then let go and walked away. Between Aunt Shelli's question and the woman's comment, it was clear to me that I *must* have come to this synagogue sometime before. But why?

Aunt Shelli and I looked at each other uncomfortably. The line wasn't even moving.

"They keep the doors shut during certain prayers," Aunt Shelli whispered to me. "They'll open them in a moment."

Someone bumped me from behind. How could there be so many people trying to get into synagogue? And it wasn't just adults—there were people my age in line, too. One really short black-haired girl I thought I recognized from my gym class last year. I'd never spoken to her before, and I hadn't realized she was Jewish.

Aunt Shelli and I kept looking at each other and looking away. I couldn't think of anything to say. I wondered if she was going to make me talk to the rabbi. And I was shocked that Papa had actually agreed to let me come. That was the craziest part. He actually told me he thought it was a good idea! I knew Nana wanted everyone to patch things up, but why did *I* have to be stuck in the middle of it?

Finally the ushers opened the giant doors, and the line began to shuffle forward. Inside, the room was packed. There had to be at least three hundred people filling up the seats, but Aunt Shelli walked right up to the front. There on the far end of the row were Uncle Steve, Micah, and two empty seats they'd saved for us. They nodded a quick hello and went right back to the responsive reading. At least it was in English.

The morning was endless. A lot of Hebrew mumbling. *Some* songs that were pretty to listen to. And a few things that I could follow, like the rabbi's sermon. He said that we might all be Jewish, but what that meant in each of our lives was something different. Some of us were extremely observant; others only came to synagogue once or twice a year. There was no right or wrong way to be Jewish, he said. But it was important to understand what being Jewish meant to you on a personal level. And to act accordingly and deliberately. "Don't let the circumstances of your life dictate your beliefs," the rabbi said. "Contemplate. Then make a choice."

I liked a lot of what he was saying—it sounded so reasonable. I wondered what he'd think about someone like me, though, who chose nothing.

THAT NIGHT we went to dinner at Micah's house, and afterward, when all the adults were in the kitchen doing the dishes, Micah and I went into the living room. I wished we could watch TV; I had no idea what to say to him after our last awkward conversation, but Rosh Hashanah was like Shabbat times ten, so no TV.

We sat on opposite sides of the couch, not looking at each other. I played a song in my head for a while, while Micah kept rubbing the palms of his hands on his khakis. I tried to think of as many possible conversation starters as I could. But I didn't know which topics were safe.

"It's strange," he finally began. "At my old school, I was in the jock crowd, but at Pershing . . ."

I bit my lip.

He sighed. "This year isn't really going the way I'd pictured it."

I smoothed my palm against the velvety fabric of the couch. He didn't seem angry, just worn down. "You kind of stand out,"

I said. "Maybe if you tried to be more like the guys on the team."

"I don't want to be like them. I want to be myself. I just don't want to be ostracized for it." Micah lifted up his glasses and rubbed the bridge of his nose. "I can't believe there's so much anti-Semitism at our school."

"What are you talking about?" I'd never seen anything like *that* going on.

"You don't think my being Jewish has anything to do with the way I'm treated?"

"I don't," I said. "If you weren't Jewish, but you acted the same way you're acting now, I think the same things would be happening."

"Really?" Micah's tone clearly suggested he didn't believe me. "Then why did you tell me not to wear a kippah?"

I sighed. I didn't want to get into that topic again. "Because it's weird. None of the other Jewish students do it." I thought about the girl from the synagogue. "I've never heard of any other Jewish students having problems."

"Right," he said. "As long as they're Jewish like you. Which means hardly at all."

His words were like little whips, lashing at me. They stung, even though "hardly Jewish" was exactly how I would have described myself. "This is only about fitting in on the football team?" I asked. "No one else has made any comments about your religion, have they? Sara thinks it's cool that you wear a . . . a . . . you know." I pointed at his head. I still couldn't say it.

He nodded. "Yeah, but Sara's not like most people at Pershing."

I could hear it in his voice. His tone changed when he said her name. I had to know if he was going to ask her out. "It seems like you and Sara have been talking a lot lately."

Micah blushed, but he didn't say anything.

"Sorry," I said. "It's none of my business."

"I didn't mean that." Micah shrugged. "She's really great, but she's not Jewish."

"What does that have to do with anything?" I asked.

Micah's cheeks flushed again, and I felt the heat creeping into my own face, too. He was talking about dating her, and it mattered that she wasn't Jewish because it meant he could never go out with her.

"Now who's prejudiced?" I asked.

He shook his head. "This isn't prejudice. Being Jewish is really important to me. How could I be with someone who couldn't share that?"

My insides were torn between relief and anger. "So . . . what? You're only going to be friends?" I asked.

"It's not that simple. I like her," he said. "But I don't know what to do. Besides, I think my parents would be really upset if I dated someone who wasn't Jewish."

"Can't you make your own decisions? You said they left that stuff up to you."

"And look where that got me." Micah leaned back against the couch, defeated.

"See?" I said. "This is why I don't want to practice our religion. It's totally not worth it."

Micah sprang up. "You're wrong. It is worth it," he said. "Even when I don't know what I should do, at least I know who I am and where I'm starting from."

That night, my conversation with Micah kept me from falling asleep. He'd sounded so sure, so confident, when he'd said that he knew who he was and where he'd come from. I didn't know those things about myself at all. I wondered if I ever would.

THE NEXT DAY I went back to school, since Nana let me follow the Reform custom of celebrating only the first day of the Jewish New Year. As I went to my morning classes, I couldn't help wondering if anyone suspected why I'd been absent. I'd told Sara, of course, but she was the only one. And it's not as though she'd have a reason to tell anyone.

On the way to the cafeteria, Hayden stepped up beside me and linked her arm through mine. "There you are," she said. "Let's get lunch."

"Oh, I . . ." I hadn't planned on sitting with them today.

"I already told Austin you were eating with us," she said. "He's saving a table. We missed you yesterday. Where were you?"

I told Hayden the same thing I'd texted Austin last night. "Twenty-four-hour flu."

"You missed all kinds of fun drama." Hayden leaned her head toward mine. "When I asked Austin where you were, Lara joked that you were probably off praying with Geekberg, and Austin told her to shut up!"

Hayden arched her eyebrows; she seemed to expect me to be happy that Austin had told Lara off for me. But my throat had completely closed. I tried to smile; only the left corner of my mouth twitched up. Austin had been offended on my behalf—was the idea of me going to services with Micah so offensive to him?

In the lunchroom, she steered me to the seats. I looked around, but didn't see Sara, Zoe, or Skye anywhere. I didn't want them to get annoyed at me for ditching them again.

Harrison spent the whole lunch hour complaining about Micah and the missed practices.

"Three. He's missing three in one week!" He looked disgusted. "It's bull that he gets away with it. Especially now that he's playing two positions."

"He's been working hard," Austin said.

"Whenever football doesn't interfere with more important things." Harrison ripped open a bag of chips.

"It's a holiday." Austin unwrapped his hamburger.

"There was a Jewish guy on the team last year. He never missed any practices." Harrison pointed at his knee, then looked hard at Austin. "You'd think Micah would realize that he owed the team, owed me, not to screw up our season."

Austin nodded. Then he rewrapped his uneaten burger and stood up. "I just realized I have some homework I forgot to do. I'll catch you guys later." He turned to me and squeezed my shoulder. "Sorry."

As Austin headed off, Sara entered the cafeteria. She saw me sitting next to Hayden and rolled her eyes. I looked down at my salad. I wasn't even hungry anymore. The only reason I was sitting at this table was to be with Austin, and Austin had study hall after lunch. He could do his homework then. So why had he left?

11

A t our next football game, Harrison sat on the bench with his own clipboard, furiously scribbling notes. He reminded me of when I was little and I'd go to the grocery store with Nana. I'd bring my own shopping list and use one of the little mini-carts the grocery store had for kids, following along behind her, feeling all grown-up.

Harrison never cheered or cracked a smile once, and every time someone made a bad play he jabbed his pen against the paper. He chewed a couple of players out, too.

At the beginning of the fourth quarter, Pershing took the lead when Austin threw thirty yards to Micah, who ran in for the touch-down, then kicked the extra point. But in the next play Madison South returned Micah's kickoff all the way to our ten-yard line and scored on the next play. Harrison took the paper off his clipboard and tore it in half. He headed off to the locker room alone, a min-ute before the game was even over.

Afterward, Harrison was waiting for Austin and me by the

Jeep. I figured he'd want to go home and rest his leg, but when he climbed in the car he said, "I'm ready to get hammered."

We turned onto Pershing Road. Micah was walking home not too far ahead of us.

"Be careful," Harrison said. "He's not wearing his special jacket."

Austin half laughed, but as we drove past Micah, Harrison grabbed the wheel and tugged it to the right. The Jeep dipped into the shoulder. A spray of gravel slapped my face, and Austin swerved left to recover. We veered into the oncoming lane for a second.

I grabbed the roll bar with both hands, my heart ricocheting around my chest.

"Holy crap!" Austin shouted as he pulled onto the shoulder again and slammed on the brake. "What was that?"

"Relax," said Harrison. "It was only a joke. You're fine. He's fine."

I looked behind us. Micah was on his hands and knees, but he was starting to stand up. He was okay. I took a deep breath and said the words to myself again. *He was okay.*

"Don't do that again," Austin said. He got out of the car and ran back to Micah. I jumped out of the backseat and followed him.

"I'm sorry," Austin was saying to Micah when I caught up to him. "I completely lost control of the car for a second. Are you okay?"

Micah wriggled his shoulders like he was stretching the kinks out and said, "Yeah, I'm fine. A little freaked out."

"Are you sure?" I asked. "Did you hurt your leg when you fell?"

Micah looked dazed. "A skinned knee. No big deal."

"Maybe I should take you to the hospital," Austin said. "At least let me drive you the rest of the way home."

Micah wouldn't accept the offer. "You guys should get back in your car before you get a ticket. You're half on the road."

"You'll be okay if we go?" I asked.

He jogged in place for a few seconds. "See? No harm, no foul."

Austin and I went back to the Jeep, but I kept my eyes on Micah as we drove away. He'd acted like it was no big deal, but it looked like he was limping.

"I told you," Harrison said. "He was fine."

"He hurt his knee," Austin answered.

"*He* hurt his knee?" Harrison shouted so loud I flinched. "That's whose knee you're worried about? It's nice to know who your friends are."

I waited for Austin to tell him that it wasn't about loyalty, it was about sanity. And trying to run over someone was insane. But all Austin said was "You're my best friend, Harrison."

When we got to Hayden's, I climbed out the back of the Jeep into a cloud of exhaust before Austin even turned off the engine. Austin helped Harrison out of the car and up the front steps with his crutches. I waited by the crabapple tree in Hayden's front yard. After a minute, Austin came back to find me.

"You okay?" he asked. He stood facing me, slowly inching himself closer.

I shook my head no and stared down at our feet. I was shaking. Austin reached out and grabbed one of my hands.

"We almost killed Micah." My voice trembled. "Harrison's crazy."

"We weren't really that close to him," he said. He kissed my cheek. Then he pressed his forehead against mine as he spoke. "It's hard for Harrison to watch someone else playing his position."

"We almost hit him," I said, but it felt like our foreheads were melting into each other. There was silence as I watched my breath cloud up in front of Austin's face and my words sink into his skin.

"I know," he said.

"But it's not okay," I said. "He can't do that."

"I'll talk to Harrison," Austin said, then kissed me. I closed my eyes and kissed him back.

"Let's go inside." He grabbed my hand, pressing his thumb into my palm, and walked toward Hayden's house. The pounding beat of the music and the smell of beer drove away any other thoughts. Austin guided me through a crowd and into the kitchen where a cooler of beer and soft drinks sat on the floor. He handed me a diet soda; I put it back and grabbed a beer. I'd never had one before, but it seemed like a good way to stop thinking about Harrison. Austin popped the cap off my bottle and held it to my lips. I took a sip. It was bitter and made my nose sting.

"Let's go find someplace private to drink these," he whispered in my ear.

Holding the bottles in one hand, Austin's other hand grabbed mine and led me down into the basement. The overhead lights were dimmed. A flashing blue haze from the television lit the room: a bunch of guys were watching a basketball game on three sofas angled around the giant-screen TV. Behind one of the sofas was a pool table, where Hayden and John Barstow, her junior, were playing a game with another couple. The walls were covered in sports memorabilia. Austin took us to a dark corner where there was a low seat, like a double beanbag chair. He flopped himself into it, then pulled me down next to him and handed me my beer.

"I'm so glad it's the weekend," he said, taking a swig.

"Me too." I closed my eyes and took a big gulp of beer, trying to still the shudder that went with it. Maybe I'd get used to it after a while. Maybe after it made me forget what had just happened.

Austin tapped the tip of my nose with his finger. "You're a million miles away," he said.

I looked into his eyes, soft and warm. Micah would probably forget all about it. Tomorrow. Or in a few days.

I took another sip of beer.

"Essie?" Austin scooted closer to me. I could smell the beer on his breath and a hint of cologne. I wanted to crawl inside his shirt. "Are you there?" he asked.

I kissed him. I'd never done that before, kissed him first, but I couldn't talk. The only thing to talk about was what Harrison had done. What we'd let him get away with.

Austin kissed me back and put his arms around me. I wiggled closer and let my brain escape into the feeling of Austin's palm against my back, not caring, maybe even glad, that everyone in the room could see. Austin liked me.

As USUAL, the next night Austin picked me up at seven. We went to the laser show at the Cranbrook planetarium. In between colored flashing lights, a Pink Floyd sound track, and a lot of hand-holding and kissing, Austin said he had something important to ask me. It sounded so official, but I couldn't figure out what it might be. "What?" I asked.

"Later," he said.

My hands shook all through dinner as I wondered what the question was. The only thing Austin asked was "Are you done with your fries?"

After we finished dinner, we drove to Orchard Lake. Austin turned the car off, but left the battery running. Hip-hop played on the stereo, and the headlights shone out over the water. This was the part of the night I'd been waiting for. Austin began kissing me and instantly I entered dreamland.

After a few minutes, he pulled away, wound his fingers in one of my curls, then let it go.

"So," he said, his voice a bit deeper than usual, "I wanted to ask you to the homecoming dance."

"Yes," I blurted, realizing as I said it that he technically hadn't asked yet. "I definitely want to go with you."

"After the dance, a bunch of people are going to the Holiday Inn." He looked down at his lap. "Do you want to?"

Homecoming and then a hotel party. Like the parties at

Hayden's, only cooler. A giant smile took over my face. But then I realized if this party was at a hotel it probably meant all night. Nana wouldn't agree to that. She wouldn't even let me stay out past eleven.

"You mean a sleepover, right?"

"Yeah." Austin grabbed my hand and looked deep in my eyes. "We don't have to."

"I'll just have to check with my grandparents," I said. I didn't want to spoil his night by telling him the truth. There was no way my grandmother would agree to me spending the night in a hotel with my boyfriend.

"Good." Austin brushed his lips against my hand. "I wasn't sure you'd want to."

"Of course I *want* to," I said. An entire night with Austin. Sleeping next to Austin. I couldn't think of anything more perfect. A tiny voice inside wondered what else we'd do, but Austin had said we'd wait, so I told the voice to be quiet.

"It's going to be a really special night," he said.

I nodded. I had to figure out a way to go.

We kissed for a while more, then moved on to driving lessons. Austin taught me how to do a three-point turn and how to reverse into a parking space. Afterward, he dropped me off at home. This time, no one flicked the porch light on for me.

"I'm home," I called, stepping inside. I could barely hear myself over the clatter coming from the kitchen. Nana and Papa didn't answer, so I guessed they hadn't heard me either.

"I'm home," I repeated, walking into the kitchen. Nana and Papa were at the kitchen table playing Boggle.

"Oh, Essie!" Nana shouted. "You're back!" She reached into the box. "Here's a pad and paper. Sit down and play with us."

I sat between them, put my hand on the timer, and waited for Papa to stop shaking the cubes. He had an intuitive shaking method. He didn't stop until he felt a good mix of letters.

"Did you have a good time?" Nana asked.

I nodded.

"He's such a nice boy."

"Good manners," Papa agreed.

It seemed like the perfect moment to ask them about the hotel party. I tried to think of the right way to phrase the question.

Papa put down the cubes. "Flip the timer," he said to me.

I flipped it and started looking for words—both for the game and for the question I needed to ask. Maybe I could tell them that the hotel was part of the official homecoming activities. Nana ran her fingernails over the back of my neck the way I loved. "You are such a good girl," she said, forgetting about the game.

The question was halfway up my throat, but I swallowed it down. I wasn't such a good girl anymore. I was illegally learning to drive behind her back. I'd ridden in a car that had run my cousin off the road, and I'd drunk a beer. I just knew that if I asked to go to the hotel, the truth about me would suddenly become clear to Nana. I couldn't ask. If I wanted to go to the hotel party, I'd have to come up with some other way.

12

I called Sara first thing Sunday morning to tell her that Austin had asked me to homecoming. Her reaction seemed genuine and positive, so I invited her to go shopping for a dress with me. Once we were in the changing room at Macy's with a stack of dresses, I told her the second part of the news. "He wants me to go to a hotel party with him afterward."

Sara bugged her eyes out at me, but I ignored her. "What do you think of this one?" I held up a navy-blue strapless sheath.

"Hold on," Sara said, grabbing the dress from me. "Are you going?"

"I don't know yet," I replied, taking off my shirt and jeans. "I'm not sure what I'd tell my grandparents."

"Forget about that." Sara took the blue strapless off its hanger and unzipped it for me. "You have other things to worry about first. Are you ready to spend the night with him? You've only been going out for a month."

I stepped into the dress, and Sara zipped it up. "It's a party. It's not like we're going to the hotel alone."

Sara looked at me like I'd just said the stupidest thing ever. "Eventually everyone's going to pair off, Essie. And that dress is too long."

She was right. It hit me in the middle of my shins; I looked like I was playing dress-up. I stepped out of it, and Sara put it back on the hanger.

"All right, so we'll be alone for part of the time. It's not like we're going to do anything. He's already said he'd take things slowly. It would be fun to sleep next to him and wake up together." I picked up the next dress to try on. It was black and sparkly with spaghetti straps. "Just because we might sleep in the same bed doesn't mean anything will happen."

"I know *you* don't plan on doing anything, but what do you think he expects? Don't forget his reputation. You should be asking him to get tested."

I was starting to get exasperated. "He's never tried anything remotely close to that with me. He knows I don't want to. He's sweet and nice, and I'm sick of you putting him down. Just because he's a cute guy does not mean he's a jerk!" I pulled on the black dress, but it was so low cut I knew I'd never be comfortable wearing it.

"I don't think all cute guys are jerks," Sara protested.

She offered me a pink chiffon. I took off the black dress and traded with her, completely annoyed.

"I don't think Micah's a jerk," she said. Her voice was soft, and I knew she was trying to avoid a fight, but it was too late.

"Yeah, well, you're wrong," I said. I put the pink dress on. It was soft and delicate with an Empire waist and flowy fabric that floated gently away from my body. I looked like a princess. "He likes you, but he'll never date you because you're not Jewish."

Sara zipped me up, then stepped back without saying anything. I looked at her reflection in the mirror. I could tell that she was hurt from the way she sucked in her bottom lip. I couldn't believe what I'd just said. I'd meant to break it to her gently.

"I'm sorry," I said, wishing I could take back the last five minutes. "I didn't mean to tell you that way. He likes you a lot. It's really complicated for him."

Sara nodded, swallowed, and blinked her eyes a couple of times. "I like this one best," she said, pointing at the pink dress. I took it off and charged it on Nana's credit card. Then Sara and I went next door to the café. We shared an iced coffee, but Sara hardly spoke. I couldn't tell if she was still mad at me, or just needed to think things over. I only knew that whatever she was feeling, she wasn't sharing it with me. Even though I knew I deserved it, it hurt. Sara was my best friend, but no one who looked at us would have been able to guess it.

AT CHEERLEADING on Monday, I told everyone that Austin had asked me to homecoming, and Hayden suggested we share a limo with her, Lara, John, and Harrison. At the end of practice, Ms. Young made us run laps. Lara, Hayden, and I ran together.

"Remember homecoming last year?" Lara said. "You accidentally sat on Vi's dress in the limo and tore it. She sulked the whole night; she was so uptight."

I nearly tripped over my feet. When I'd seen Austin in the hall with Vi last year, he'd seemed to really care about her. Now she was nothing more than an annoying memory for Lara. Would I become that, too?

"Run much?" Lara asked me.

"Bitch much?" Hayden said with a laugh, making it sound more like a joke than anything else.

"Are you guys going to the hotel after the dance?" I still didn't know what I was going to do.

Lara gave me a look that said "What's it to you?" but Hayden nodded. "I'm counting every second. John and I are saving our-selves until then."

I stumbled again.

"What is wrong with you?" Lara looked down her nose at me, but before she could say anything else, I interrupted, "So are your parents okay with the whole hotel thing?"

"Completely," Hayden answered. "You know how laid back they are. They're the ones helping everybody get the rooms."

"Mine aren't laid back at all," Lara said. "But what they don't know won't hurt them, right?"

"What do they think you're doing after the dance?"

"Sleeping at Hayden's."

I nodded and thought over her words during the last lap. When we finished, we jogged back over to Ms. Young and she told us to hit the showers.

A plan was becoming clearer and clearer in my mind, but I couldn't believe I was even considering it. I could ask to sleep at Sara's after homecoming. Nana and Papa always let me sleep at Sara's, no problem. They'd known her parents my whole life. Not that I'd really be sleeping there.

One more thing to add to the list of secrets I was keeping from my grandparents.

I wondered if Sara would be okay with it. Lying for me. Covering for me if they called. I couldn't see it happening, especially after yesterday. It would be easier if I could tell Nana I was sleeping at Hayden's like Lara, but Nana would call Hayden's parents to introduce herself. She never let me sleep at someone's house unless she knew the parents. If she thought I was sleeping at Sara's, she wouldn't check in at all.

It had to be Sara's, even though Sara would never go along with it. But maybe she didn't have to know. It's not as if it would even affect her.

ON THURSDAY, I was supposed to go to services with Aunt Shelli. Again. There was another Jewish holiday; this one was called Yom Kippur. According to my uncle it was the holiest day of the year—a time to fast and ask for forgiveness for your sins.

I didn't want to go. First, there was no way I could go a whole day without eating while listening to old men mumble in Hebrew. Second, at practice on Wednesday I'd overheard Lara tell Hayden that Micah was missing more practices, making it three last week, plus two this week. She said he was letting the team down, that he didn't even care about homecoming or making it to the playoffs. I didn't want her to start complaining about me, too.

Instead of getting dressed up for synagogue, I went downstairs to breakfast in jeans and a hoodie.

"Why aren't you wearing something nice?" Nana asked as

she put a plate of waffles down in front of me. At least she didn't expect me to fast.

"Nana, I don't want to miss any more school. I have a math test next week. And homecoming is coming up. It's really important that I be at today's practice."

Nana studied me, and I could tell she was thinking my words over. Finally she nodded. "I'll call Shelli and explain," she said.

"Thank you!" I took a sip of my milk—Nana didn't let me drink coffee—relieved to have gotten off so easy.

"We are still going to break the fast with them tonight," Nana said.

"But we're not fasting." I held up a forkful of waffles.

Nana brought me the bottle of syrup. "When your father and Steve were boys, before they were old enough to fast, I used to tell them that children only had to fast from junk food on Yom Kippur."

I almost choked. Nana had mentioned my father. She barely ever did that. Even though I was always glad to get any details about him that I could, she'd caught me off guard. Plus, there were so many things about that sentence that were hard for me to imagine. My father and Uncle Steve as boys. Nana celebrating a Jewish holiday.

She'd raised her own children Jewish, but not me.

I didn't know what to say, but Nana wasn't waiting for an answer. She seemed lost in her thoughts. I reached to pour more syrup, but she opened the bottle and poured it on my waffles for me. Then she began to cut them into pieces.

"Nana!"

She looked at me, startled, as though she had no idea why I'd shouted. I pointed at my plate. "I can cut my own waffles."

"Oh!" Nana laughed, put my knife and fork down, and sat next to me. Her words had gotten me thinking, and I decided to risk a question.

"Were you and Papa ever observant?"

Nana rubbed the back of my hand and stood up. "Not like your aunt and uncle are now, but they weren't so observant back then, either."

"Why didn't you raise me with religion?" I didn't want to follow as many rules as my uncle, but for the first time I wondered what it would have been like to have had even a little religion in my life.

Nana's face went slack. "Who told you to ask that?"

"No one." I shook my head, confused. "It's just something I keep thinking about lately—you know—how different my life would have been if I'd been brought up like Micah." Would I be a different person?

The color faded from Nana's face until she looked so sickly I thought she might faint. "Would you have preferred that?" she asked.

"No." I answered automatically, before I really thought about her question. It wasn't an issue of preference. I was just curious.

"I needed you, Essie. I needed you with me. You were the only thing I had to hang on to when your parents died. I couldn't even mourn. Papa wouldn't let us sit shiva, wouldn't talk to the rabbi, didn't even want them buried in a Jewish cemetery. He felt so betrayed. But your uncle! He grew his beard and tore his clothes. He went to synagogue three times a day, and even when the official mourning period was over, he fixated on Judaism. He wanted to learn everything about it, to observe every last ritual, to the exclusion of everything else in his life. And he became so judgmental of everyone who couldn't find that same comfort. It was his way of grieving. I know that now," she said, pressing her fingers to her lips. "We did what we thought was right at the time, but we were all acting in pain. That's what you have to understand."

Nana left the room and I knew for certain she'd be spending most of the day in bed, though she hadn't done that in such a long time. I turned to my breakfast and shoveled in a huge bite, feeling terrible for bringing so much pain to Nana. But shaky and excited and scared, too. Nana had given me more glimpses into my past in this one conversation than she had in my entire life. What did she mean when she said that she needed me with her, that I was the only thing she had to hang on to? And she did what she thought was right. What did she do? What happened after my parents died that nearly tore apart the rest of my family? What would it do to Nana if I tried to find out?

THAT NIGHT AT MICAH'S, dinner wasn't until nine. We had to wait until there were three stars in the sky to start eating. Even though I hadn't been fasting, I was starving by the time food was served. We all sat down to bagels and lox and something called kugel, a noodle pudding that tasted much better than it sounded.

After dinner, Micah was excused to catch up on schoolwork, so I went into the kitchen to help Nana and Aunt Shelli with the dishes, while Papa and Uncle Steve went into the living room to talk business.

Aunt Shelli cleared, Nana washed, and I dried.

"Essie's going to her first dance," Nana told Aunt Shelli as she placed a pile of plates next to the sink.

"You'd better take pictures," Aunt Shelli called out as she went back into the dining room.

"Nana, I wanted to ask you something," I said. She handed me the first wet dish, and my hand shook as I took it. "After the dance, could I sleep over at Sara's? Austin will drop me off at her house."

Nana held out a bowl, and I put the dish I'd been drying on the counter so I could take it.

"I don't know," she answered. "Going over to her house so late?"

"It's not *so* late," I objected, turning the bowl around in my hands. They were trembling so much I worried I would drop it. Nana *had* to notice. "I want to be able to talk to her right after the dance is over."

Aunt Shelli came back into the kitchen with an armful of plates. She looked at me as she set them down next to the sink, then walked back out of the kitchen without saying anything. I wondered if she was listening to our conversation.

"Won't Sara be asleep already?"

"Nana! She and Zoe and Skye might even go to the dance." They'd joked about it the last time I'd eaten lunch with them. Which was a while ago, but still. "And if they don't go to the dance, they'll go to a movie or something. She won't be asleep."

Nana nodded as she scrubbed the bottom of the kugel pan. She was starting to come around.

"Please." I begged. "Sara's my best friend. I want to be able to tell her everything that happens."

Nana relented. "All right. It's a special night." She handed me the wet kugel dish. "I guess it'll be okay."

I took the dish and began to dry, telling myself how great the night would be. But the surge of excitement I'd been expecting to feel never happened. The more I thought about it, the more I realized that the lie I'd just told my grandmother was partly true. Sara was my best friend, and I *did* want to share this night with her. But she probably wouldn't want to know anything about it.

13

Barely a week had gone by before we had to go to Micah's for dinner *again*. For another Jewish holiday. I couldn't take a breath without inhaling one. They were everywhere. This time we were celebrating Sukkot, a Jewish harvest holiday where people build little huts in their backyards. That meant another missed practice for Micah. I was surprised he was willing to keep missing them. I wondered how his teammates felt about it. The Panthers had lost another game the previous Friday night. Coach took Micah out after the first half, but his replacement wasn't any better.

The sukkah in Micah's backyard was a wooden cube with canvas mounted on three sides to make walls. The ceiling was made out of leafy branches, but it wasn't that sturdy; I could see patches of orange-blue sunset right through it. My uncle said we were supposed to see the sky. That was one of the rules of sukkah construction. The evening was clear and crisp, comfortable enough to eat outside, which was good because according to Jewish law we were actually supposed to eat in the sukkah.

I was surprised when Sara showed up. Apparently Micah had

invited her, and she hadn't told me she was coming. How could she not tell me? And how could she be so calm around Micah? I'd fall to pieces if I had to be around Austin all the time without being his girlfriend. But maybe Sara wasn't going to talk to me about that kind of stuff anymore.

Besides Nana, Papa, Sara, and myself, there were some people from my aunt and uncle's synagogue: that woman I'd seen on Rosh Hashanah, and several others who were thrilled to see Nana and Papa. Apparently Nana and Papa had once belonged to Aunt Shelli and Uncle Steve's synagogue. And Nana and Papa seemed happy to see everyone, too. Papa even wore a kippah without being asked. Lately it seemed that everything I had assumed about my grandparents and religion was getting turned inside out.

We stood together at the edge of the sukkah and watched while my aunt lit two tall candles. The flames danced in the breeze. My uncle said blessings over wine and bread, and we all ate a piece and drank wine from tiny Dixie cups. Then Micah did this thing where he shook a big bumpy lemon and some branches. My uncle explained that though we weren't required to shake the etrog (lemon) and lulav (branches), he thought it made the evening more special. He wanted everyone to take a turn. The crowd broke up, and he began calling people over one by one.

Sara and I moved to the edge of the sukkah and I rolled my eyes at her. "Can you imagine having to do this kind of stuff all the time?" I whispered.

"I think it's interesting."

"That's because you can go home and forget about it. There isn't a sense that this could become your whole life."

She shrugged. "Don't be melodramatic. It's not going to become your whole life, either. You can learn about your religion without having to believe or practice every bit of it, you know. And it's a part of who you are even if you don't follow it. Even if you don't know about it. So isn't it better to know?"

"My grandparents didn't think I needed to know about it." I thought about Nana's comments the other morning, but shrugged them off.

"Yeah, Essie, but you're your own person. What do *you* think?"

"I think my life was fine before." I left the sukkah and sat down at the patio table.

Sara followed me. "I'm just telling you how I see things. I grew up like you. It's not like my parents taught me anything about Christianity. But when I watch Micah's family, I feel like I'm missing out on something. I don't mean being Jewish—just having any religion."

I put my hand on Sara's forehead. "Are you feeling okay? What happened to the old Sara?"

She didn't answer, and Micah came out and asked us if we wanted to shake the lulav. Sara was really into it. She asked Micah's father questions about the history of the tradition, too. Then my uncle handed the branches to me, three different kinds bunched together. "You recognize that?" he asked me, pointing to the one in the middle.

I raised one eyebrow at him. "Should I?"

"It's hadassah. Myrtle branches."

Huh? I had no idea what my uncle was talking about.

"Queen Esther's Hebrew name was Hadassah."

"Oh," I said, feeling stupid because he acted like Queen Esther was someone I should know all about. All I knew was that she was someone in the Bible.

When everyone had had a turn shaking the lulav and etrog, the adults crowded around the buffet. I didn't feel like elbowing my way in, so I went to sit on the swing set. Sara followed me. We each took a swing, and when Micah noticed us he came over and sat down on the grass in front of Sara.

"This holiday is amazing," she said to him. "I love the idea of celebrating the harvest. Everyday things like apples actually are sacred when you think about it."

"I know what you mean." Micah smiled up at Sara, but the smile wasn't in his eyes. He lay down on the grass and sighed.

"You okay?" Sara asked.

Micah glanced over at his father, who was absorbed in conversation with Nana. "Well, things were starting to get a little better," he said. "I mean, at least the guys on the team don't act like I'm not even in the room anymore. Then on Monday, someone poured pop in my cleats while I was in the shower, and today . . ." Micah's face turned deep red. "Somebody put Icy Hot on . . . on some of my equipment."

This was not something I wanted to know about my cousin.

"That's hazing!" Sara scooted to the edge of her swing like she wanted to jump up and arrest somebody. "You have to tell."

"Tell who? Coach? What am I supposed to say? I don't even know who did it." Micah glanced at me. "I have no *proof* anyway. Besides, it's not hazing if it's just one guy."

Sara turned to me. "Do you know anything about this?"

"No!" How could she think that? So I hadn't exactly told people he was my cousin, but it's not like I would do anything mean to him. I'd even stuck up for him a couple of times.

A fly buzzed around my foot. I watched it land on my shoe and crawl over my laces. The truth was, the more I thought about it, the more it seemed like I might know who'd done it. Micah probably did, too. "If I had to guess, I'd say it was Harrison," I said.

Sara nudged Micah's leg with her foot. "I bet it *was* him," she agreed. "Maybe you could ask Austin, Essie? He might know. Then we could go to the coach."

My insides recoiled. Ask Austin to get his best friend in trouble? What if I was wrong?

"Austin doesn't know anything," I protested. "I'm sure of it."

"Well, I'm sure, too," Micah said. "It was Harrison."

"If you're not going to complain about him, you should at least do something," Sara said. "So he knows he can't keep pushing you around."

"Such as?" Micah sighed. "Steal his crutches?"

Sara laughed. "I can think of something else I'm tempted to do with his crutches!"

Micah laughed, too, then Sara and Micah stared at each other for a moment, as if thoughts were passing between their minds. Suddenly, I didn't feel like I should be part of their conversation. I didn't think they wanted me to be part of their conversation.

I stood up. "I'm going to get some dinner. Do you guys want me to bring you anything?"

They shook their heads without unlocking their eyes, and I walked away.

FRIDAY NIGHT'S GAME was hugely important. If we didn't win, we had no shot at making the playoffs. We needed to win all of our last three games. The opposing team, Washburn, was really good. At first, I didn't think we had a chance against them, but their best running back was out with a groin pull. Washburn was ahead for most of the game, but late in the fourth quarter Austin drove Pershing down to Washburn's twenty-five-yard line. With two seconds on the clock, he called a timeout. We were only down by one, 14–13. The crowd was chanting, "Per-shing! Per-shing!"

I sat on the sidelines, the grass cold and damp against my knees and a nervous fluttering in my chest. It was hard not to get wrapped up in the action of close games. The whistle blew. Micah and the field goal team jogged out onto the field. It was a long field goal—longer than Micah had ever kicked in a game before, and I didn't think he'd make it.

Micah rocked back and forth on his feet a few times, mumbling his field goal prayer. Finally, he took three steps backward, moved to the side, then took one, two, three steps forward, and let his kick fly. The ball sailed through the uprights clean and easy. Around me the cheerleaders were jumping, screaming, and shaking their pom-poms. Two more wins and we could make the playoffs.

The players poured out onto the field, pumping their fists in the air. Sean and Keith grabbed Micah and carried him on their shoulders. Soon they were surrounded by everyone on the team and the cheerleaders, too. Everyone but Harrison. He sat on the bench alone, staring out into the end zone.

I turned back to the celebration. I was the only cheerleader who hadn't joined them yet. I walked up to the screaming team looking for a friendly face, but everyone was packed so tightly together, I couldn't find a place to fit myself in.

WHEN THE BUS dropped us back at school, I waited outside for Austin by his car. Sara was standing by the fence. The night was cold. Her bright yellow hat and scarf stood out against the dark.

"Hey," I said. "What are you doing here?"

She buttoned up her coat and stood up straighter. "Oh, hi. I didn't think I'd see you. Where's Austin?"

"Still in the locker room. Where's your car?" I asked, looking around the parking lot.

"Zoe dropped me off after the game," she said. "I'm going to walk home with Micah."

"You're going to walk home with Micah?" I pictured Sara and Micah on the road, shoulders touching but not holding hands. I could see Harrison reaching for the wheel. Rocks spraying them both.

But Austin wouldn't let it happen again.

"I can tell what you're thinking," she said. "But you're wrong. We're just friends."

"No," I said. But I couldn't tell Sara my real thoughts. "I don't want you to get hurt." It was the essence of the truth, anyway.

"You don't need to worry about me." Sara laughed. "I'm the one who worries about you, remember?"

Sara looked over my shoulder and waved. I turned and saw Micah appearing out of the darkness. "Good game," I said.

He shrugged. "It's my job." He turned to Sara. "Hey there."

"Don't feel too bad," she answered, elbowing him in the ribs. "Maybe you'll lose the next one."

Micah laughed. They smiled at each other like they had some inside joke. It made me feel off-kilter, my cousin and my best friend sharing things I wasn't a part of. But then, I had things I didn't share, too. Maybe that was the way it had to be.

"Do you want us to wait with you until Austin comes out?" Sara asked.

I shook my head. "I'll be fine." I wanted to give them a head start on the road.

Sara and Micah headed off, and for a while I heard their voices softly floating back to me.

Austin and Harrison came out a few minutes later. On the way to Hayden's, Austin slowed down and moved to the center of the road as he drove by Micah and Sara.

Harrison shouted out the window, "Rabbi's gonna get laid."

HARRISON'S COMMENT kept me up late after Austin dropped me off Friday night and it was the first thing on my mind when I woke up Saturday morning. What if Sara thought I was like Harrison now? That Austin and I were laughing at his comment as we sped past her and Micah? I hoped that she knew me better. I didn't even like Harrison. I didn't really like any of Austin's friends. *Sara* was my real friend, and I wanted her back. Things felt so strained between us lately. I fished my cell phone out of the pocket of last night's jeans and called her to see if she wanted to hang out.

"Sorry," she said. "I can't today. I'm busy."

I waited for more, but that was it. No further explanation.

"Okay. How about tonight?" I asked. Austin's parents were making him spend the night in Ann Arbor with his brother.

"I have plans tonight, too."

Since when was Sara's schedule so overwhelmingly full? And since when did her plans have to be so mysterious? I was starting to get annoyed. "How about tomorrow, then?"

She paused, and maybe sighed. I couldn't tell. It might have been a bad connection. "I'm really sorry," she said. "I've got something to do then also."

"That's it? That's all you're going to tell me?"

"Sorry," she said again. "There isn't anything more I can say."

Suddenly it dawned on me what was going on. Sara was blowing me off. She was finally letting her feelings about Austin and all his friends come between us. Anger bubbled inside me.

"You know what," I said, my voice thick with as much sarcasm as I could manage, "I hope you have a great weekend. Oh, and don't bother picking me up for school on Monday," I added. "I'll get a ride with Austin."

"Essie, come on, don't be that way."

"What?" I didn't back down. "You obviously don't want me around."

"Don't blame this on me. You've been looking for an excuse to stop being friends ever since you first started hanging out with

Austin's crowd." Sara's voice sounded angrier than I'd ever heard it.

"That's completely untrue! You're just jealous."

"Jealous? Austin is using you, and his friends are enjoying the show. How can you be so blind?"

My eyes stung. "If I don't see everything exactly the way you do, I'm blind?"

"I can't fight with you about this. You have every right to be friends with whoever you want, but so do I."

"Have a nice life." I snapped my phone shut. For a moment I felt completely righteous and satisfied. Then loneliness set in and all I wanted to do was call Sara back, but I couldn't. She didn't want me anymore.

14

I moped around for the rest of the day and spent Saturday night in pajamas letting Nana teach me to play bridge. Or try to teach me. I couldn't really concentrate. Sunday morning, I plopped myself down on the couch, unable to care about geometry and chemistry homework. I planned to watch TV for the entire day, since I had no one to have plans with. Austin was still with his brother. I'd called Hayden but only got her voice mail, and she never called me back. And now that Sara and I were split, I figured Zoe and Skye were her friends, not mine. Watching so much TV meant I was going to have a major homework marathon at the end of the day, but I wasn't ready to break up my pity party.

I clicked on the TV for my day of vegetation and was taking a bite of my banana when Nana came in wearing a tracksuit.

"Aunt Shelli will be here in fifteen minutes," she announced. "Go get ready."

"Ready for what?"

"She called while you were sleeping. She wanted to know if

you'd like to come to her dance class. I told her yes. It'll be good for you to get out of the house."

"Nana! No." When would Nana ever stop making plans for me? I didn't want to go to synagogue with Aunt Shelli again.

Nana kissed me on the forehead as though she hadn't even heard me.

"Papa and I are going to a senior yoga workshop," she said. "Go get ready." Then she was out the door, and I dragged myself upstairs to get dressed.

WHEN THE RED MINIVAN pulled into the driveway, Aunt Shelli climbed out, but left the motor running. I opened the door before she could ring the doorbell. Aunt Shelli looked surprised and laughed.

"I guess you're ready, then," she said. "Good. I wasn't sure if you'd want to go."

Did she really think I wanted to go?

"Where's Micah?" I asked, locking the front door.

"Working on a school project, I think. He wouldn't give me any details. But I wanted us to have some alone time." Aunt Shelli put her arm around my shoulder as we walked back to the car. It was a little weird because I still didn't know her *that* well. I didn't put my arm around her, but I didn't wriggle away, either.

"So," Aunt Shelli said, when we got to the car. "Aren't you about the right age for driver's ed?"

I wondered if Nana and Papa had said anything to her. "I decided to wait until I'm older," I told her, even though Nana had made the decision for me.

She looked at me sideways. "Oh. Do you want to talk about that?"

"No," I said, jerking away from her more abruptly than I'd meant to. Her arm dropped back to her side. I thought Aunt Shelli had moved back to patch things up with my family. Did she want me to break Nana's heart?

"Sorry," I said. "I meant no, thank you."

"I understand," she said. "But if you change your mind, I'm a very good listener."

I nodded, and we both got in the car. At the synagogue, Aunt Shelli pulled a rolling suitcase out of the backseat and I followed her inside into a room filled with rows of folding chairs. Kiddie play equipment was stacked along one wall. I started moving the chairs out of the way, and Aunt Shelli unzipped the suitcase and pulled out a CD player.

"Do you know anything about Israeli dance?" she asked me as she plugged it into the wall.

I shook my head no.

"I'm sure you'll have no problem picking it up. None of the dances we're going to do are that complicated. Well, they won't be complicated for you. Wait until you see Mrs. Leibovitz. I think she has *three* left feet!"

A chubby, balding man with a boyish face walked up to us and kissed Aunt Shelli on the cheek.

"Essie, this is Larry Rosen, the president of our synagogue. Larry, I'd like you to meet Essie. She's my assistant today," Aunt Shelli said.

"Glad to see you," Larry said to me, reaching out to shake my hand. "I love when members of the youth group participate in synagogue activities."

It surprised me that he just assumed I was part of the synagogue. I thought about telling him that I wasn't, but something stopped me.

Over the next five minutes, more and more people walked in and my cheeks ached from smiling as I was introduced to each and every one of them. They were all so happy to see me, like they were starved for teenagers. After my lonely weekend, it actually felt nice to be wanted.

"Okay, everyone, we'll start with a hora to warm up." The entire group formed a circle and Aunt Shelli put on some old-fashioned, gypsy-sounding music. She grabbed my hand and pulled me into the circle, too. "It's just a grapevine step until the music changes, then we'll walk into the center and back out again."

I began crossing right over left, right behind. Two times around and I knew which woman Mrs. Leibovitz was. Although the dance was pretty basic, the music was kind of peppy and I added a jump to my step as we marched into the center and back again. After sitting on the couch for so long, it felt good to be up and moving.

After the hora, we did another circle dance with a name I never caught. This one was a bit more complicated, with a lot more jumps, changes of direction, and one part where we stopped and danced with a partner. After that Aunt Shelli taught us a line dance she'd made up herself called Shake Your Bagel. It reminded me of the Macarena with belly-dance moves. By the end of the class, I felt light and peaceful. I realized I hadn't felt that way in weeks.

Aunt Shelli came over and gave me a hug. I was a little bit

sweaty; my shirt stuck to my back where her arms had been. "That was fun," I said.

"I'm so glad you thought so. You can come back anytime you like."

I nodded, but I didn't promise anything. I didn't want to get carried away. It was better than sitting by myself watching TV, but I couldn't see myself hanging out at a synagogue *every* Sunday morning.

On the way home, Aunt Shelli said, "I know we're just getting to know each other again, Essie, but I wanted to tell you something."

Aunt Shelli glanced over at me, then back at the road. She seemed so serious my mouth went dry. I nodded my head at her, to let her know she could go on, even though she wasn't looking at me.

"I don't how much you know about what happened after your parents died . . ." Aunt Shelli's eyes flicked over to me again, and nerves took hold of my chest.

"Not too much," I said. "Nana and Papa don't talk about it."

Aunt Shelli nodded slowly. "Well then, I'll just say that I always wanted a daughter of my own." Her voice cracked slightly on the word *daughter*. I looked up, and her eyes were shiny. "That wasn't meant to be." She coughed. "I hope we can become close one day, but even if that never happens, I want you to know that I'll always be there for you, whatever you need."

"Thanks," I said, but I wondered if I would ever feel that connected to Aunt Shelli. It seemed like the kind of relationship she was talking about would need to have begun when I was younger. How could we start now? I thought about telling her what I used to imagine, like I told Micah, but I couldn't. Even thinking about it made my chest feel swollen and heavy. So instead I tried to smile at Aunt Shelli, to show her that I appreciated her offer. The smile only came out halfway.

MONDAY WAS the first day of my new driving arrangement. When Austin picked me up for school in the morning, Harrison was sitting in the front seat. I'd forgotten we'd be driving with him, too. It didn't even feel like I was going to school; the whole thing was so strange. I'd never gone to school without Sara. Before she got her license we rode the bus together. In the backseat I felt invisible. Austin and Harrison hardly spoke to me. They spent the whole ride talking about Stevenson High School's quarterback.

As we got close to school, my phone buzzed. I practically ripped my backpack open to get it. Maybe Sara wanted to apologize. Maybe she hadn't really been blowing me off. Maybe her mom had been in the room and she just hadn't wanted to give details about her plans. But when I opened my phone, I didn't recognize the number. And it wasn't a text message or a voice mail. It was a photo with the subject heading "Pershing's New Secret Weapon."

I opened the picture, and there was a guy wearing a purple-and-gold bra and women's underwear with fishnet stockings. The guy was posing sexily in the locker room with one leg up on a bench. When I looked closer, I realized it was Harrison. Or it looked like Harrison. The face was definitely Harrison's. But was the picture real? I couldn't imagine Harrison ever putting any of those things on.

Of course it wasn't real, I realized. Harrison's knee was injured. It was just really good Photoshopping. And then I realized something else. Sara was taking a digital media class. Was this what she'd been doing all weekend? With Micah?

Harrison would go ballistic if he found out about the picture. I flipped my phone shut as we pulled into the school parking lot. I wondered how many people had seen it. When we got inside, I kept watching for people checking their phones, or smirking at Harrison, but I didn't notice anything. I decided not to say anything to Austin. Maybe they had only sent the picture to me—although the number hadn't been one I recognized. I didn't know who actually sent it. Austin and I said goodbye by the drinking fountain, and I went to class, trying not to feel too sad about the fact that Sara and Micah might have done this together without telling me. I'd never know one way or the other, anyway, because I couldn't ask her.

BY LUNCHTIME on Tuesday the whole school had seen the picture. Most people thought it was hysterical. Except for Harrison. He sat pushed back from the table with his leg propped on a chair in front of him and his arms folded across his chest. A vein bulged in his temple.

"You should wear that outfit to the game on Friday," Sean said. "Stevenson will be so distracted by your body they won't be able to concentrate."

Harrison didn't answer. He shot Sean a look that bordered on serial killer, but Sean didn't notice or care.

"Lay off," said Austin.

Sean ignored him, blowing Harrison a kiss. "You're so sexy when you're angry."

Harrison grabbed his crutches and stood up. "When I find out who did this, that person is going down." He stared hard at each person at the table, then stalked off.

Sean grabbed Hayden's nail polish from the table. "Did you forget something?" he called after Harrison.

"Hey!" Hayden squealed, trying to grab it back. She couldn't manage very well because her nails were all wet.

Lara stood up and plucked it from Sean's hands. "You are such a slime," she said. I wondered if she would go after Harrison —to comfort him or something, if that was even possible. But she didn't. She handed the nail polish to Hayden and sat back down, but Austin got up.

"What's the matter with you?" he asked Sean.

"It's funny," Sean said.

"I'm going to go talk to him," Austin told me. I nodded, though I really didn't want to be at the table without him. I reminded myself I had no one else to eat with anyway. I watched Austin walk past Micah and Sara's table.

At least Micah had gotten his payback, and I didn't have to feel guilty anymore. Sara hadn't needed me to talk to Austin. That is, if Micah was really the one who'd sent the picture. I just still couldn't believe Sara and I weren't friends anymore.

I looked across the cafeteria. Sara was showing Micah and

Skye something in her sketchbook; they probably didn't care that I wasn't sitting with them.

No one at my table was even talking. Hayden was still doing her nails. Lara was on her cell phone and Sean was shoveling his burger in his mouth without coming up for air. I wished Austin was still here. Without him, I felt untethered. As though any second I could float up to the top of the cafeteria and get stuck behind one of the steel beams like a balloon from last year's prom. And who in the cafeteria would even know or care that I was gone?

15

Even though I hadn't given Nana the new driver's ed form, and I'd told Aunt Shelli I wasn't going to learn how to drive, the truth was, Austin was still giving me driving lessons. I loved the feeling of being behind the wheel of a car, how grown-up and different and in control it made me feel. I couldn't keep doing it, though. Every time Austin gave me a lesson, I promised myself it would be the last time. We only drove in deserted parking lots after dark, but still, it was risky. Someone could find out.

And then Austin changed the rules. He wanted me to drive him to the homecoming game. At first I said no. Driving in secret was one thing; driving on the actual street was another. What if I got pulled over? Austin was really persuasive, though. He lived less than a mile from our school. It'd give him more time to focus on the game. It'd be good for me.

He was impossible to resist. I agreed.

By the time I turned Austin's Jeep into Pershing's lot, I was frazzled beyond belief. The whole ride I'd worried that the police were watching my every move, ready to bust me for underage driving any second.

"Jeez." Austin laughed as I eased into a space with no cars on either side. It wasn't his spot. "I bet your grandparents drive faster than you."

I turned off the ignition. My fingers hurt from gripping the wheel, but the thrill of having done it was starting to take over. "It's not fair of you to complain about my driving when you're the one making me do it," I said.

"Well, somebody has to. Only five more months until you're sixteen."

For some reason, he had decided that I *had* to get my driver's license when I turned sixteen. He was even bugging me to sign up for the next session of driver's ed. I'd let him teach me, I told him, but no driver's ed. I wasn't going to get my license.

"Shouldn't you focus your energy on something else, like, maybe . . ." I cocked my head to the side and wrinkled my brows like I was thinking really hard. "Um . . . I don't know . . . football?"

"Ha. Ha." Austin shook the kinks out of his shoulders. "How am I supposed to concentrate when I know you're on the sidelines watching me?"

"That should make you play better." I grabbed my bag and climbed out of the car.

Austin followed me. "Well, it would," he said, "if I had an incentive."

"I can't promise anything," I teased. "Let's see how well you play first." I skipped ahead of him, my brain buzzing with the thought of what he might say next.

"Nice. Really nice," he said. His footsteps pounded behind me as he ran up, grabbed my waist, and lifted me into the air.

"Put me down," I screamed, but his arms around me felt warm and safe.

"Uh-uh," he said, readjusting his grip. "First you have to tell me what my reward is if we win tonight."

A funny feeling rose up in my throat. I gulped it down, kicking my legs a little, and squirming like I wanted him to let go.

"I could make you a certificate," I offered. "Best Quarterback."

Austin shook me from side to side. "Come on. You can do better than that!"

"A kiss?"

"Okay, we're improving, but I want something even bigger."

My breath caught in my chest, and I coughed. His arms around my waist felt too tight. I tried to loosen Austin's grip. He lowered me to the ground and let go.

"Austin, I'm not ready yet." I kept my back to him and my eyes on the ground. My whole body was rigid with expectation. Let him be okay with that, I prayed.

"Nobody feels ready at first, Essie." Austin put his hands on my shoulders. I wanted to rest against him, but I couldn't. Not until he said it was okay. "You just have to do it anyway. It's part of life."

Was he going to make me do it? Would he break up with me if

I couldn't? My body trembled. I couldn't make this decision in a parking lot. "Can we talk about it later?"

"You've been putting this off forever!" Austin spun me around and grabbed the sides of my arms. "I wouldn't push you to do this if I didn't think you were ready."

Was he right? Was I ready?

"Promise me, if we win, you'll turn in your driver's ed form on Monday."

"What?" I shook my head, trying to clear my thoughts. "You were talking about driving lessons?"

"Sorry. I couldn't resist. But seriously, what's the big deal? It's just driver's ed."

The panic and fear that had been building up inside me in response to that other question, the one he didn't ask, exploded. "I just don't want to," I said. "Why is it such a big deal to you? What do you care if I drive or not?"

Austin took a step away from me. The playful light in his eyes faded. My anger evaporated.

I should have told him about Nana. How I could never do that to her, how she needed me to be her little girl. But it was too hard to explain. I wasn't like other girls who were supposed to grow up and rebel against their mothers. I had to stay who I was so Nana wouldn't lose me.

"I'm sorry," I said.

"I was just trying to help you," he said, avoiding my gaze. "Most people can't wait to get their driver's license. It's the first step to freedom. I want you to have that." He gave me a quick peck on the cheek. "I'll see you after the game." He headed into school.

"Austin?" I called after him.

"We're cool," he said, but he kept walking toward the school without turning around.

Harrison was leaning against the brick wall outside the doorway, his crutches lying on the sidewalk. He wore a pair of jeans with a button-down shirt, a tie, and his varsity jacket. He looked pretty pissed off at something, but he straightened up a bit when he saw Austin.

"Hey," Harrison said, his voice thick.

Austin just grunted and continued on into school. Harrison slouched back down and fiddled with the tip of his tie. I guessed he didn't want to be with his team while they were putting on their uniforms. Not when he couldn't wear one. I stood on the sidewalk, not knowing what to do. I couldn't follow Austin all the way into the boys' locker room, and none of the other cheerleaders would be at school for a while.

"Trouble in paradise?" Harrison asked.

He seemed to be talking to his tie, but I figured the question was for me. I didn't want to answer it.

"You're all dressed up," I said instead. "Why aren't you wearing your jersey?"

"The jersey's a joke. I slashed it. So my dad made me wear this." Harrison deepened his voice in imitation of his dad. "'If you're not suiting up, you dress to show your team some respect.'" He banged his fist against the wall. It made him lose his balance for a second. "Why should I give them respect? No one's giving me any!"

Even though I couldn't wait to get away from Harrison, a part of me felt bad for him. It had been five days since the picture started circulating, and the gossip about it hadn't died down yet. I'd even seen it posted in the stalls of the second-floor girls' bathroom. And Austin told me someone had sent the picture to Harrison's dad. He hadn't taken it well.

"I'm sure all the guys appreciate your support." I couldn't believe how lame that sounded, but it was the only thing I could think to say.

"Right."

Behind me I heard footsteps. Micah was walking across the parking lot. His face remained expressionless as he noticed me first, then Harrison.

"Hey," Micah said to me as he walked past. Harrison gave him a look of disgust.

"Good luck," I answered. Then Micah went inside.

"I'd like to shove his beanie down his throat," Harrison mumbled. Then he pounded the back of his fist against the wall again. There was so much anger in him I could almost see it exploding out of his hands. I flinched, and took a step away from him.

"He's never even apologized." Harrison glared at me. "If it wasn't for his lame-ass kick, I'd still be playing. And I'd probably have a college scholarship."

He bent over and yanked at the Velcro on his brace. The ripping sound made me jump. "He doesn't even care about the team." His eyes glazed over. I couldn't tell if he was talking to me or to himself. "I think he's the one who sent the picture."

I took another step backward. I didn't want to hear any more. I

knew Austin wanted me to be patient with Harrison because of all
he was going through, but this was getting uncomfortable.

"I'm going to go wait for the cheerleaders." I had an hour
before anyone else came, and Harrison probably knew it, but I
couldn't stand there with him another second. I turned around
as fast as I could and went back to Austin's car. I still had his
keys; he'd rushed off before I could return them. I turned on the
radio, found some music with a good dance beat, and tried to let
it fill me with energy. My mind clouded with thoughts of Austin,
Harrison, and Micah. It felt like forever before the game would
begin.

THE HOMECOMING FLOATS were lined up on the track behind the
football field. They made the field festive, but the noise from the
crowd was filled with anticipation, not celebration. People stood
six deep on either side of the bleachers. It looked like double the
fans we usually had. It sounded like triple. I could hardly hear our
music over the screaming. We managed our opening cheer anyway, and my body felt electric. The roar from the crowd drowned
out every earlier worry. I saw the team gathering at the far end of
the field. I had a great feeling about this game.

I faced the stands to cheer as the announcer introduced the
teams. I went crazy screaming when he called Austin's name.

We kicked off first, and Micah's kick was kind of short. Stevenson returned to the fifty-yard line, but couldn't go any further. We
stopped them on downs, and then it was our ball. Even though the
night was cold, our cheers rising up with vapor trails, my palms

were sweating around my pom grips. I couldn't believe how much I wanted Pershing to win.

Stevenson had a great offensive line, but our defense was getting the job done. Thank goodness, because Austin hadn't found his rhythm yet. At the end of the first quarter, the score was tied 0–0.

In the second quarter, Austin's passing game was hot and Micah scored our first touchdown minutes before the half. Stevenson broke out in the third quarter and scored three touchdowns. We just couldn't get close enough to the end zone to match them. Micah kicked two field goals, though, one at the end of the third quarter and one at the beginning of the fourth, but later he missed an extra point. I could hear Coach yelling at him about that one, even though I was halfway down the field.

With three minutes to go in the game, we were down 21–19. But we had the ball and were moving it along. All we had to do was get within field goal range. The other cheerleaders and I had practically shouted ourselves hoarse. My throat burned.

With forty-three seconds left, we still needed to get about fifteen more yards to get close enough for Micah to try a long field goal. The players lined up for the play. Keith snapped the ball. Austin dropped back, found Micah, and released the ball. My stomach clenched, and I stood up on my toes as though I was going to catch the ball myself. Micah caught it, and even over the cheers I could hear the crunch-and-thud of the tackle. Austin called a time-out. Micah limped back to the bench.

The team gathered around Coach. We had the ball on the twelve-yard line, and it all came down to Micah.

It wasn't a very difficult field goal, and I wondered if everything would change for him when he made it. He'd be the hero of the game. Maybe he'd finally be accepted.

When the timeout was over, the field goal unit took the field. Micah stood behind Keith, looking limp. Usually before a kick, he was ready to spring and rocked back and forth on his feet, building up energy. He must have been especially nervous, so much was riding on the kick. He didn't even do his prayer thing.

Micah took such a deep breath you could see his shoulders rise and fall. He took three short steps back, then two big steps forward, and let his kick go. I jumped up as the ball sailed straight on toward the goal post, my cheer ready in my throat. But then the ball curved left. I squeezed the handles of my pom-poms. *Let it be good.*

The ball hit the left upright and dropped to the ground. No good. My hands went clammy.

Cheers erupted from the stands. It was Stevenson. They knew they'd won. Micah walked off the field without lifting his eyes from the grass. No one said anything to him when he sat down on the bench. Any hope for the playoffs fizzled. The season might as well be over.

16

After the game, the group at Hayden's house was small: just me, Hayden, Lara, Sean, Austin, and Harrison. We piled onto the sofas in Hayden's basement and began to pick apart the loss. I sat on Austin's lap.

I tried to concentrate on Austin's hand resting between my knees. To think about all the time we'd have together without the football crowd now that the season was effectively over. But Austin virtually ignored me. I felt invisible. Everyone else was talking about the game, trying to figure out what had gone wrong, but I didn't want to add to their conversation. Maybe because I was the only one who wasn't drinking.

"I feel like getting totally wasted," said Hayden, taking a gulp of her wine cooler.

"I know," Sean said. "It hasn't sunk in yet. I really thought we had a chance."

"We *did* have a chance." Lara looked around the room, making eye contact with everybody one at a time.

I kept my eyes down and traced my finger along the top of my beer. Austin always got me a beer now when we were at Hayden's, but tonight I just pretended to sip it. It was warm, and the taste nauseated me, like I was drinking sweat.

Everyone else in the room was on their third or fourth drink at least. And the more they drank, the more it became clear to them that the team had been on a downward spiral ever since Micah's crappy kick made us go into overtime in the third game, the game when Harrison had been injured.

Harrison sat on the beanbag in the corner of the room. He was the only one, apart from me, who wasn't saying anything. Every time I looked over at him, he was staring down into another beer. Now he took a long, slow drink, his hand gripping the can like it was someone's neck. It made me squirm, but I couldn't look away.

Sean let out a huge burp. "This bites."

"I know," Lara agreed. "You guys worked so hard all season, then one guy messes it up for you."

"He didn't even look like he was trying to make it." Sean popped open another can. "It was like he only half kicked."

Lara nodded, and Hayden said, "Yeah."

Suddenly, I wished that Austin would take me home instead of making me listen to this conversation. I didn't want to hear any more about Micah. It wasn't fair. He was a decent guy. He never should have tried out for the football team—he didn't fit in with these guys. Now that the season was nearly over, I wished they'd leave him alone.

"We should do something," Harrison mumbled.

"Did you say something?" Sean asked. I think he was as

shocked as I was that Harrison had finally spoken. But then Harrison turned to us and repeated his words.

"We should *do* something."

I half hoped he meant do something like go to a movie or play pool, but I knew he didn't.

Hayden jumped up from the couch. "Wait! Wait! I have the best idea!" She ran into the storage room and came back carrying this giant white thing that she plunked down on the coffee table. It was a megapack of toilet paper.

"Jeez, Hayden." Austin laughed. "Do you have some intestinal issues we should know about?"

"Very funny." Hayden put her hands on her hips, and my stomach wavered, like I was the one with a digestive problem. "The boy said let's do something, so . . . here's something."

"That's nothing," Harrison said. "What else do you have?" Harrison got up and hobbled into the storage room.

"Does anyone know where he lives?" Sean asked. We all knew who he was talking about.

I know, I know, I know, my brain chanted. I pressed my lips together and prayed that Austin was too drunk to remember. *I couldn't tell them. It's not like toilet-papering a house was *that* big of a deal, but still, I couldn't tell them.

"I know where he lives," Harrison announced, coming back out of the room with his shirt bulging in front.

"Let's go," Sean said.

Lara stood up, then swayed back and forth a few times before she was completely steady. Hayden bumped into the couch twice as she tried to walk around it, and Sean bumped into me. Some of his beer sloshed onto my arm.

There was no way I would get into a car with them. I could picture us all unconscious, bloody cuts on our faces, in a car wrapped around a telephone pole.

I squeezed Austin's leg. He'd realize they shouldn't be driving. He was careful about stuff like that. He usually never drank more than one beer, and often didn't even finish it. But he'd had way more than that tonight.

My head spun; I tried to make it go still, to think. Think of some way to stop this from happening.

Lara and Hayden put on their coats. Austin stood, knocking me off his lap. He took a roll of toilet paper and wrapped it around his head like a turban. I tried to catch his eye, but he didn't notice me. Were they really going to do this?

A voice in my head kept saying, *Stop them, stop them.* But I didn't say anything.

I thought about Hayden's parents upstairs and nearly cried with relief. They'd stop us. But then I remembered. They'd poked their heads downstairs to say good night a while ago.

"Can we all squeeze in your van?" Austin asked Sean.

Sean shook his head. "We'd fit, but there's no way I can drive."

My eyes misted with relief. Sean knew he couldn't drive. Maybe they'd all realize they needed to hang out a while and sober up.

"Is anyone good to drive?" Hayden asked.

No one, thankfully, said yes.

"Essie's good." Austin pulled me up from the couch and put his arm over my shoulder. "She barely drank at all, and I've been teaching her to drive." He let his hand drop down to my hip and squeezed me to him in a way that made it seem like teaching me to drive meant more than it really did.

My cheeks flushed. I stepped away from him. "I can't drive Sean's van."

"It'll be fine," Austin said. "You can do it."

"But all I've driven is your car." I grabbed Austin's hand and tried to will my thoughts into his brain. *Everyone's drunk. Don't ask me to do this. I don't want to drive.*

Austin stared back at me like he truly heard me. He shrugged. "Okay," he said. "I'll drive. I've only had a couple of beers. I'll be fine."

Sean tossed Austin the keys, and Austin walked toward the stairs. His foot tripped on the first step, but he grabbed the railing and kept going. Hayden carried the pack of toilet paper as the rest of us followed them.

I couldn't let Austin drive, but if I woke Hayden's parents, we'd all get in trouble. They were fine with us having a beer or two in the safety of their house, but they'd never be okay with us drinking and driving. They might call the other parents. Everyone would hate me, including my boyfriend. Not to mention what my grandparents would think of me.

What if I called Nana and Papa?

Nana would never let me see Austin again.

So that left one option. I had to drive. And assuming that I didn't cause a terrible car accident or get pulled over and arrested, I was driving to Micah's house. What if his parents came outside and saw me?

I couldn't think about that. I'd have to hope for the best.

———

I PUT THE KEYS into the ignition and turned on the van. It was huge, not even a minivan. A van-van. Austin sat up front with me and everyone else climbed into the back rows. Lara popped open a beer from the six-pack she held on her lap. I didn't see how it would be possible to get out of this night without something horrible happening.

I looked around for the gearshift. If anyone noticed that I was taking forever to back out of the driveway, they didn't say. They were talking about the time they had TP'd Keith's house last year.

Finally, I put the van in reverse and pushed on the accelerator. We lurched backward. My stomach jumped up into my mouth, and I slammed on the brakes. Everyone in the back cracked up, and Austin said, "Just keep going. It's straight all the way to the street."

I clenched my teeth and looked over my shoulder. I couldn't do it. I didn't know how to drive a van. I wanted to scream and cry and turn off the ignition, to get out and slam the door. But if I did that, then one of them would drive. I pushed the gas pedal again, lightly at first and then with more and more pressure until we reached the street. Then I took a deep breath. I'd made it out of the driveway.

At the end of Hayden's street, I turned onto Orchard Lake Road and headed south toward Micah's. Emptiness settled down on me. The closer we got to Micah's street, the more hollowed out I felt. No one seemed to wonder how I knew which way to go. Lara was telling everyone about the Special K diet she was on.

I imagined Micah and my aunt and uncle waking up tomorrow

morning and finding the mess in their front yard. Maybe they'd see it as a joke. I hoped.

When I turned onto Micah's street, Harrison called out, "Kill the lights."

I twisted the gear stick, but the windshield wipers went on. "Shoot," I said.

Hayden and Lara began laughing hysterically.

"Pull it toward you," Sean said.

I pulled it, but wound up flashing the brights, not killing the lights. My fingers went rubbery.

"Stop driving." Harrison's voice was deadly cold, and I did what he said.

Austin reached over and turned off the headlights.

"Now," said Harrison, "drive as slowly as you can and park near the corner. Everyone be quiet."

The only sound was my heart thumping. I parked in front of a red brick house with a white picket fence that looked gray in the moonlight. We tumbled out of the van. Only one house at the end of the block had its porch lights lit. But when my eyes adjusted, I realized that it really wasn't dark enough. If anyone peeked out their windows, I was sure they'd see us.

"Let's go," Harrison whispered. He went up the sidewalk without looking back. Hayden, Lara, and Sean trailed after him. I couldn't believe this was really happening.

"Wait," I said, grabbing Austin's arm.

Austin turned around and stepped right up to me so that the fronts of our jackets were touching. His breath smelled like beer and felt steamy compared to the October night air. I took my hands out of my pockets and put them around his waist. He hooked his thumbs into the back of my jeans and stared into my eyes. Micah's house was a million miles away.

When Austin kissed me, reality disappeared. The cold air, the fear, Harrison and everyone down the block, everything evaporated. Nothing existed but Austin and me.

This is what it feels like to be in love.

The thought made me open my eyes. I tilted my head back, and Austin opened his eyes, too. He smiled at me like I was the only person on the planet. I pulled my arms around him even tighter. I wanted to be closer to him than I'd ever been before. Even this didn't feel close enough.

Austin ran his fingers through my hair and pulled my face to his. His kiss was as soft as a butterfly, and it made my heart ache. I wanted to climb back into the van with him and ignore what was going on down the block.

"Let's go," Austin whispered, lacing his fingers through mine and leading me down the sidewalk.

My body rebelled. I couldn't let go of Austin's hand, but my feet wouldn't move. *Let's stay,* I thought.

"Come on," he said, grabbing my other hand. His eyes locked with mine, and I took a step.

"I feel funny about this," I said, my breath frosting in the air as I spoke.

Austin's cheeks were flushed pink from the cold, but his eyes were warm. "It's no big deal."

I sniffled; my nose was beginning to run. "Yeah, but what about Micah?"

"He'll have to spend the weekend cleaning up his yard." Austin kissed me. "Just like I did my first year on the team."

"You did?"

"It's just a prank, Essie, really. A way for Harrison, and all of us, to let off some steam." He rubbed the back of my hand with his thumb. "So are you coming?"

My brain clouded for a moment with the fog of indecision. All I could think of was what Sara would say if she knew what I was considering. How horrified Nana would be. But they didn't have all the facts. They expected me to feel some big connection to Micah that wasn't there. But my connection with Austin was real. If I had to choose between them, the choice seemed obvious.

AT MICAH'S HOUSE, the big oak tree next to the driveway already dripped with white ribbons. Lara and Hayden were spraying Silly String on the bushes by the front door. Sean was draping the shrubs, but Harrison wasn't there. I looked around the yard and couldn't see any sign of him.

Austin grabbed two rolls of toilet paper from the pack on the sidewalk and handed one to me. "We'll do that one," he said, pointing to the tree at the edge of the yard. Austin unwound the paper a bit, then pulled his elbow back like he was about to throw long.

I squeezed the roll in my hand. It was the soft and fluffy kind of toilet paper. I twisted my wrist around and let it unravel a little bit. Even Austin's house had been toilet-papered. It wasn't a big deal.

Just before I threw, I heard the shuffle of footsteps coming from the side of the house. Harrison walked back to the front yard looking smug.

"Where were you?" Austin's voice was a loud whisper. I looked behind Harrison, not sure what I expected to see. The flagstone path along the side of the house was all that I could make out.

"Had to take a leak," Harrison answered.

Sean let out a laugh, then covered his mouth when he realized how much the sound carried. "That beer just goes right through you," he whispered.

Harrison grabbed the rest of the toilet paper and went to help Lara and Hayden with the hedge on the side of the yard.

I wiggled my toes in my shoes. They were starting to feel numb. I shivered, and hoped we didn't stay too much longer. I could feel the temperature dropping.

I backed up a few steps and looked at the crabapple tree. Austin was on his second roll of paper, but the tree only looked about half-covered.

"Are you saving that for something special?" Austin winked, pointing at the roll in my hand. I still hadn't thrown it.

"Now you're in trouble," I said, keeping my voice low. I cocked my arm back and threw the toilet paper at his head. It sailed by him, wide by about two feet.

Austin shook his head at me. "That was the most pathetic thing I've ever seen." He picked up my roll and brought it back to me. Putting his hand on my hips, he turned my body sideways and spoke softly in my ear.

"Point your front arm toward the tree, to where you want the paper to go." He put his hand under my elbow, and I tried to concentrate on his instructions. "Now pull this arm back. Try to throw it up and out."

I kept my hands where he put them, and glanced back at him over my shoulder. "Ready?"

"Whenever you are."

I heaved the paper as hard as I could. It flew to the tree, hit a branch on the right, and dropped with a thud, leaving a twirl of paper dangling above it. Austin picked me up and swung me around. "Nice throw!"

Next door, a light went on in an upstairs window. I froze. My eyes darted to Micah's house, expecting someone to burst out the front door.

"Grab everything, but don't run." Harrison glided past us on his crutches. He moved so smoothly it was like they were a part of his body. Austin and I picked up some empty tubes and followed him to the van. I wanted to run as fast and far away as I could go. I imagined some faceless neighbor peering out onto the dark street, wondering if he'd heard something more than just the wind. Would he call the police? I shook off the thought. Not for a prank. No one calls the cops for a prank.

We climbed back into the van. Sean said he was okay to drive. I was shivering so badly that I let myself believe he was. I sat in the backseat and closed my eyes. My curfew had come and gone a half hour ago, but Papa had a cold. Nana told me he wanted to go to bed early, that I should wake them up when I got home.

When Austin finally dropped me off, it was almost midnight. Just like I'd expected, Nana and Papa were sleeping. I crept upstairs and slipped into my bed. In the morning, I'd pretend I'd forgotten to wake them. That their little girl had been safe in her bed since eleven.

17

I woke the next day with my head throbbing. My sleep had been full of crazy dreams. I was at school driving up and down the hallways in a bumper car. Harrison was spraying me with Silly String. I tried to find Austin, but I kept crashing.

I dragged myself out of bed and went downstairs for a glass of juice. I needed to wash away the ickiness of my dream and start thinking about homecoming. The dance was only ten hours away.

"Essie, get dressed," Nana said, walking into the kitchen. "We're going out." Her voice was anxious and impatient, like she was angry at having to ask me the same question a hundred times. But it was only the first time she'd asked.

"Now?" I took a sip of my juice and checked the clock. It wasn't even nine yet.

Nana's brows pinched together, and she was all hunched over. She was in no shape to go anywhere. But she didn't need trouble from me. I put my glass in the sink.

"Where are we going?" I asked.

"Lois Stewart just called. She was out walking her dog and saw police cars at your uncle's house. Their front yard is a wreck, and they're not answering their phones. I've called three times!" Nana's voice cracked, and my spine stiffened. "You'd think they'd pick up in an emergency."

There were police cars at Micah's.

A hot neon sign plastered itself to my face. *I did it!* it flashed. My skin tightened, like the outside of me was shrinking. "Are we allowed to go over there on a Saturday?" I asked.

"Get yourself ready to go." Nana took a deep breath, and gave me a look that said, *Not another word.*

"Do you think anyone is hurt?" Nana asked Papa in the car.

Hurt? I thought. *Why would anyone be hurt?* Fear trickled down my spine.

If anything bad had happened, it was my fault. I could have stopped it. I could have woken Hayden's parents, or called Nana and Papa. Or even told everyone that Micah was my cousin. Maybe the surprise would have distracted them.

It hadn't even occurred to me to tell the truth.

Please let everyone be okay.

We turned onto my cousin's street, and sure enough two police cars were parked at the side of the road. The yard looked like a mummy had exploded. It was kind of pretty in way, but then I noticed the words EAT SHIT, RABBI spray-painted on the front door. Had that been there last night? How had I missed it?

Papa parked our car behind the second police cruiser, and I slouched down in my seat. I didn't want to get out.

186

What if I had to talk to the police? The officers would know the truth the second they saw me. They were trained to spot a person who was hiding something. They could arrest me for being an accomplice. Or maybe I wasn't just an accomplice. I'd thrown toilet paper. I was guilty.

Nana and Papa got out of the car and rushed into the house without me. It was like they'd forgotten I was there. I didn't follow them. The front door of the house opened again, and three police officers, two men and a woman, walked out. I crouched down even further, hiding myself. When I heard the cruisers drive away, I opened my door and climbed out, desperate for fresh air.

I wandered under the trees dripping with toilet paper, and pulled on a ribbon. It broke off halfway up, leaving a strand too high in the tree to reach without a ladder. The pressure of tears built up behind my eyes, but I tilted my head back and blinked to keep them from falling out. It would take forever to clean this up. I knew I should go inside and offer to help. But I lingered on the lawn staring up into the kaleidoscope of white.

When I finally opened the door to my aunt and uncle's, I was hit with Uncle Steve's shouts. "How can you say any part of this is my fault? They smeared feces all over the patio! Not to mention the brand-new furniture and grill that are destroyed!"

I closed my eyes and shut the door quietly behind me. I didn't go farther into the house. They were all in the living room; no one could see me.

I heard Papa's voice, low, calm. "You shouldn't have made him so different."

"You think this couldn't have happened to you? To Essie?

Because you pretend you're not Jewish? I've got news for you. The world is not as accepting as you think. And if this is the way the students at Pershing are, it affects Essie just as much as Micah."

"Don't," Nana pleaded. "Don't fight. You are not enemies here."

"Maybe if there weren't self-hating Jews like you, there wouldn't be skinheads at my son's high school."

"Let the police do their job," Aunt Shelli said. "Maybe there are no skinheads. Maybe it was just one crazy kid."

"Wake up, everyone!" Uncle Steve shouted. "It's always more than one crazy kid! Maybe one kid sprayed our door, but other kids stood by while he did it."

I heard footsteps stomping. A second later Micah stormed into the foyer. He stopped short when he saw me. A searing flush fanned out over my face, my chest, and my scalp.

Micah bit his lip as he looked at me, like I was a virus he was studying under a microscope. I chewed my pinkie nail and waited for him to call everyone in from the next room and tell them that he'd figured out that I was the one who'd trashed their house.

"So, what do you think, Essie?" he asked, squinting his eyes at me. "Skinheads or one crazy kid?"

From the sarcastic tone of his voice, I figured he knew who the crazy kid was. How much else did he know? I tried to swallow, but my throat was dry, like someone had shoved a wad of toilet paper down my esophagus.

I shrugged. "It could have . . ." My voice rattled. I cleared my throat. "It could have been anyone."

Micah looked at me like he wanted to spit on my shoes. "Is that what you really think, Essie? That there are so many people at Pershing who would do something like this? Would you?"

I blinked, stunned. My mouth opened but nothing came out.

"You know how I told you I used to imagine what it would be like if you were my sister? Well today, for the first time, I'm glad my parents lost you in the custody battle."

Micah pushed past me out the door and left me dazed in the entry-way of his house. *Custody battle?* I was so shaken I didn't even hear Aunt Shelli come into the room.

"Essie? I didn't know you were here. Are you all right?" she asked, laying a hand on my shoulder. "You're trembling!"

I couldn't speak. Aunt Shelli and Uncle Steve had wanted custody of me? "I think I need some air," I said. I opened the door and threw myself outside. Aunt Shelli didn't follow me. She had to know what I'd done. It wasn't possible that I could do something so awful and still seem like the exact same person on the outside.

I looked around at the crazy scene in the yard and began to pull paper from the trees and bushes until I had a pile up to my knees. Nana and Papa came outside and said it was time to go home. But I couldn't look at them the same way anymore. I'd assumed that my parents had chosen them as my guardians. What if that wasn't true?

WHEN WE GOT HOME, I went to my room and shut the door. The homecoming dance was just hours away, but all I could think about was Aunt Shelli. She'd been so excited about her new patio furniture, and now it was destroyed. How could I have let it happen?

All these years, I'd thought they'd moved to New York without giving me a second thought. That they didn't even remember I existed. But they had wanted me. Maybe they moved away because Nana and Papa had convinced a judge that Aunt Shelli and Uncle Steve shouldn't have me. Maybe they had convinced a judge that there was something wrong with the way they would raise me.

I went to my closet and pulled my old stuffed giraffe down from the top shelf. I hadn't slept with it for years. I didn't even know why I still had it. I'd thrown it away once, but Nana pulled it out of my trash and stuck it up in my closet. I hugged my giraffe close and pressed my nose into his nubbly neck, trying to imagine myself at six years old, when I'd never had a problem that a hug from Nana couldn't fix. Now I couldn't even *tell* Nana my problem. I couldn't tell anyone.

Tears began to leak out of the corners of my eyes. I wiped at them with my giraffe's nose, but they wouldn't stop coming. I tried to keep quiet, though—I didn't want Nana coming into my room asking for explanations.

I was making such an effort at silence that I jumped when my cell phone rang. My first thought was that it might be Austin, so I raced to answer it. I had to tell him what had happened. I found my phone on the third ring.

It was Sara.

"Hello?" My voice shook when I answered the phone. I couldn't believe how nervous I was to talk to her.

"Hi," she answered. "I'm calling about Micah's house."

I didn't know what to reply. I was sure *she*, more than anyone else, would know the truth.

"I know things are weird between us right now, but I don't know what else to do," she said.

"About what?" I braced myself for her lecture, knowing I deserved every word of it.

"This whole thing with Micah's house is my fault," she said.

What? I tried to process her words. This was the last thing I expected her to say. "What do you mean?" I asked. "How could it be your fault?"

"The picture." Sara let out a noise that was half-sob, half-moan. "I made Micah do it. He never would have sent it, or even made it, if it hadn't been for me. I thought it would teach Harrison a lesson."

A part of me wanted to confess everything to her. I didn't want Sara to feel guilty. It probably would have happened whether or not she'd sent the picture around. "It wasn't your fault," I said.

"Do you know who did it?" she asked. "If you know something, you could tell me. *I'll* go to the police. I won't even bring your name up. I have to do something to help make this better. Please, Essie. I can't live with myself if I don't."

I should be feeling exactly like Sara. I should be doing everything possible to make it up to Micah and my aunt and uncle.

"If you said something," she continued when I didn't answer, "then maybe it would make Micah willing to talk to the police, too."

"He hasn't said anything to the police?" I asked, ashamed at how relieved that made me feel.

"He told them he doesn't know anyone who could have done it. It's some kind of lame macho code of honor thing. He can't rag on his teammates, as if they'd ever do the same for him! I think he doesn't want his dad to say I told you so about trying out for football. But don't tell him I said that."

"Right," I said. As if Micah would ever talk to me again.

"The thing is," Sara went on, "I don't think Harrison did this by himself."

"You don't?"

"Come on, Essie! Do you really want to protect the kind of people who would do something like this?"

My heart stopped.

What would happen if I told her? Sara would think even less of me than she already did. She'd *really* never want to be my friend again. And no one in Austin's crowd would talk to me. I'd become a social outcast. Not to mention my family. Everyone had wanted me once, but no one would want me if they knew the truth.

"Come on, Essie." It felt like Sara wanted to reach through the phone and shake me. I closed my eyes. I wanted to tell her so badly it hurt, but it was too late.

"It's obvious that it was guys from the team! Was it Austin? Are you seriously protecting him after what he did?"

"It wasn't Austin!" I said.

"But you know who it was, don't you?" she asked softly.

"I don't," I lied.

"Think of Micah!" she shouted. "I can't believe you are covering for those jerks. Is this the only way Austin will like you?"

"Stop!" I couldn't take any more.

"Fine," she said. Her voice was flat. "I get it. You're not saying anything. Maybe you do belong with your new friends."

Clutching the phone to my ear, I sank to the floor, curling up around my giraffe. I didn't know what to do.

Austin *did* like me. I knew it. Sara didn't have the first clue about our relationship. And what good would telling the police do Micah now? His house had already been trashed. If I told, I'd get a bunch of people in trouble for making a stupid mistake, and they'd all *hate* Micah. Plus they'd hate me, too. And how in the world would that help anything?

I could hear Sara breathing, waiting for me to finally do the right thing and answer her questions. But I couldn't speak.

"Well, that's all I have to say, then," she said. "If the old Essie ever wants to talk, she knows where to find me."

Sara hung up. I didn't move. I didn't ever want to move. I'd just lie on my bed until my body rotted. That seemed about what I deserved.

18

I tried to wrap my mind around everything that had happened, but I think I was still in shock. The truth about what Harrison had done to my uncle's house kept slipping out of my consciousness as Micah's revelation took over my brain. There had been a custody battle? Over *me*? Why? I'd go over a thousand different scenarios, and then they'd all fade away in a fog as I remembered that I'd helped trash my cousin's front yard. Because of me, my aunt's patio furniture was destroyed. I couldn't focus on either situation long enough to get any clarity. I just drifted around my room like a ghost, not knowing who to talk to or what to do next.

At around four in the afternoon, I was sitting on my bed in my bathrobe. My new dress was hanging in my closet, but I couldn't bring myself to put it on. All I could think about was Harrison and Austin and Micah and Aunt Shelli and Uncle Steve and Nana and Papa.

Someone knocked at my bedroom door.

"Who is it?" I croaked.

"Aunt Shelli," came the muffled voice.

Sweat began to pour from every gland in my body. She must have come to confront me.

"Come in," I called, turning so my back was to the door.

"Hey," she said softly, sitting down on the side of my bed. "Nana said you haven't come downstairs since this morning."

"I wanted to be alone."

She scooted closer to me and rubbed my back. "Nana is beside herself. She's worried you're sick. She's ready to make you stay home from the dance." Aunt Shelli looked over at my closet. At my dress. "But I guess you're still planning on going?"

I didn't say anything. I couldn't read Aunt Shelli's tone. Was she telling me I didn't deserve to go?

"I think I know what kept you upstairs," Aunt Shelli said. "And we need to have a talk."

Oh no. She was going to call me out right now. In a way, I was relieved, but I knew it was going to hurt when she told me that it was a good thing I'd never become her daughter.

"Do you want to tell me anything?" she asked.

I turned around to face her and a sob shook my body.

Aunt Shelli hugged me to her, stroking my head and letting me cry. Then she asked quietly, "Does this have something to do with what happened to my house?"

I nodded, and my tears flowed again. My breath became ragged, and I wanted to curl into her, but I didn't move.

"Yes" was all I could say.

"Oh, Essie," she said, grabbing my hand and threading her

fingers through mine. "You don't have to worry about us. The synagogue organized a clean-up crew and our insurance company will cut us a check. Our house will be as good as new."

Aunt Shelli gazed at me with the same expression of love she'd had at our first Shabbat dinner. "I know it was scary," she said. "But it's not something that will ever happen to you. I don't want to you feel afraid of that."

I tried to make sense of Aunt Shelli's words. There was no anger in them. No accusations.

I felt ten new kinds of horrible at the thought that she was trying to comfort me. She'd come over because she cared about me. Me. The person who'd totally betrayed her. And she had no idea what I'd done.

"Come on," she said. "I don't want this to ruin your special night. Your first dance. It's going to be immortalized in pictures. You don't want a red nose." Aunt Shelli laughed.

It didn't seem right to accept her comfort. I didn't deserve it. On the other hand, maybe she was helping me make my decision. She said it herself. They'd survive. They were moving forward. Maybe I should, too.

I took a deep breath. Austin and I could have easily stayed in Sean's van that night. As a matter of fact, the vandalism had probably happened before we'd arrived. So it wasn't like Austin and I were responsible. Maybe I should tell Aunt Shelli. But a part of me worried that it wouldn't make enough of a difference. I'd still been part of the night, and if Aunt Shelli knew, she'd probably walk out of my room and never look back. I didn't want her to go.

I suddenly realized I liked having an aunt. I wanted to have her in my life.

I sat up. "I'll try," I said.

"Good for you," she said. "You are too strong a person to shut yourself up with fear."

I walked over to my vanity for a tissue and blew my nose. "I'm not strong." I was the polar opposite.

"You are. Like Queen Esther, your namesake."

"It's just a name," I said. Then I remembered Uncle Steve mentioning her to me, too. "I don't really know who she was," I added.

"Esther was the queen of Persia. She risked her life to save the Jewish people from destruction, and we celebrate her during the Purim holiday." Aunt Shelli stroked my cheek. "Some rabbis say that parents don't name their children; they simply discover what the child was meant to be named. I believe that. You've gone through so much in your life, and look how well you've handled it."

Not well at all. I was nothing like a queen. Unless there was such a thing as a queen of secrets. "I think my parents made a mistake."

Aunt Shelli shook her head. "Esther means 'morning star.' You were born in the early hours of Purim. That's why your parents named you Esther."

I couldn't believe that I'd lived almost sixteen years with this name and had never known that story. I'd thought my name was just a name, but now it felt like a mystery. My parents had called me Esther for a reason, and I never knew it.

"Aunt Shelli? Were my parents very Jewish?" Without meaning to, I asked the question in a hushed voice. Like I expected the answer to reveal some mystical secret.

Aunt Shelli tilted her head in thought. "That depends on what you mean by 'very Jewish.' They weren't as observant as your uncle and me, but they were spiritual people. They loved their religion. Your parents were the youth directors at your synagogue—our synagogue. They were coming home from a retreat when the accident happened."

"I didn't know that," I said, sitting down at my vanity. "I mean, I knew that they were coming home from a weekend out of town. I didn't know the youth director part. Or that we were members of the synagogue."

Aunt Shelli stood up behind me and put her hands on my shoulders. "I think they would have wanted you to know," she said.

I met her eyes in the mirror. "Do you think they would have wanted me to be raised with more religion?" I held my breath, waiting to hear what she'd answer. Would she realize what I knew?

Aunt Shelli's eyes grew very sad. "I think they would have wanted you to be surrounded by the love of everyone in your family," she said. "However you were raised." A lump bloomed in my throat, but I swallowed hard and wouldn't let it rise.

Aunt Shelli ran her fingers lightly over the magazine sitting open in front of me. Hairstyles and makeup tips for homecoming. She and I stared at each other in the mirror. She gathered my hair in her hands and pulled it up into a loose bun with curls framing my face and neck. The lightness of her touch made me want to close my eyes.

"How about trying an updo for the dance?" she asked. "I think that always looks nice when you are dressing up." She fiddled a bit more with my hair and said, "Something like that?"

It was red carpet hair, but it also looked soft and sweet. I liked it. I nodded, and Aunt Shelli held my hair in place with one hand and loaded in the bobby pins with her other. When all my curls were secured, she added two sparkly pins at the front of the twist and gave me a light dusting of hairspray.

"You just want a little hold," she said. "Hair like this," she said, tugging one of my curls, "needs to be able to move."

I turned my head from side to side to see my hair from every angle. Aunt Shelli had done a really good job. "I love it," I told her.

"Makeup next?" she asked.

"Yes, please," I said, but couldn't say more. The lump was still fighting its way up my throat. Aunt Shelli was being so nice to me. Nicer than I deserved. She gave me credit for being so much better than I was. Her house was the least of it. What about the way I'd treated Micah all along?

"Which one?" she asked me, pointing to the different instructions in the magazine.

"Smoky eyes," I said. Nana had grudgingly given me permission to wear makeup, and she'd even taken me to the store, but I had to pay for it all myself.

Aunt Shelli got to work, sweeping a dark color across the bottoms of my lids, layering the lighter green in the middle and then a shimmery gold on top. She didn't wear tons of makeup herself, but she was able to make it look exactly like the picture.

"Well, what do you think?" Aunt Shelli asked.

There was something wrong. The eyes were perfect, sexy and dramatic, but I was staring at a stranger. It was frightening. I couldn't connect the face in the mirror with who I was inside.

"I like it. I think," I said to Aunt Shelli.

"It's very mature," she mused. "You do look beautiful."

"Thanks." I couldn't stop staring at the stranger's eyes.

Aunt Shelli glanced at her watch. "We've still got a bit of time. If you want, we could take this off, try a different look, and then you could choose between them. What do you think?"

It couldn't hurt to see another look, just for comparison. I agreed.

Aunt Shelli turned my chair away from the mirror. "I don't want you to see what I'm doing. It will be a fun surprise."

She gently wiped the makeup off with a cotton ball, then lightly dusted something on my eyelids and cheeks and put gloss on my lips. My whole face was made up in minutes. She turned my chair back to the mirror.

It was me. Only with a little sparkle above my eyes, an extra bit of rosiness in my cheeks, and shiny lips. I smiled at myself. I liked it. Aunt Shelli was watching me in the mirror. She squeezed my shoulders. "Stunning."

I felt embarrassed for a second about how much makeup I'd originally wanted to wear.

"Another reason you are like Esther," she said.

"Huh?"

"I believe the story goes that when Esther and all the other maidens in Persia were called before the king as potential brides, she was the only one who didn't wear makeup. She let her natural beauty shine, and that's what made the king notice her. You have that same kind of natural beauty. The kind that comes from inside."

"Thank you," I said as the doorbell rang. Austin. My shoulders shivered for a second when I realized that this was it. The night was about to begin.

"I have to get back home," my aunt said. "I'll go down and tell everyone you'll just be a minute."

"Thanks."

"Essie." Aunt Shelli grabbed my hand and locked eyes with me. "I want you to remember, even though you are very beautiful, just like Esther, that's not all you are. The beauty and strength on the inside is what makes your star shine."

My aunt was being kind of sappy, and I was glad no one else was around to hear it. But I liked it, too. She was still looking into my eyes, and suddenly I remembered the strange expression on her face that night, clearing dishes, when I asked Nana if I could sleep at Sara's—like she knew what I was really planning.

"Trust your heart, and you'll always make good decisions." She kissed me on the cheek and left me alone in my room to wonder what she knew.

AFTER I PUT ON MY DRESS, I glanced in the mirror one last time. I'd never looked so grown-up.

I heard Papa and Austin talking in the foyer, but their voices were muffled. I stood in my doorway. My house looked different from the perspective of three-inch heels. I looked back at my bedroom, resisting the urge to check the mirror again. I needed to go downstairs. Austin was waiting for me.

"Here she comes," Papa announced.

"Wait, wait." Nana rushed over, camera in hand. "I want one of you on the staircase."

I paused in the middle of the stairs. Austin stood behind my grandmother and smiled up at me. He'd gotten a haircut.

"Okay," Nana said. "Come on down now, and I'll get one of you and Austin together."

I wobbled the rest of the way down and grabbed Austin's boutonniere off the hall table. Nana took pictures of us exchanging flowers, and Papa went over the night's schedule.

"Dinner at Tonelli's?"

"Torelli's." Austin squeezed my hand.

"Right, Torelli's. Then the Pershing Community House for the dance. And after?"

"Um . . ." Austin cleared his throat and looked at me, confused. A blush crept up his cheeks. I'd never seen Austin look that flustered; I hoped he wouldn't blurt something out.

"Then Austin will drop me off at Sara's house for a sleepover," I said, keeping my eyes on the floor.

"What a long night!" Papa shook his head.

"Are you *sure* you want to stay out so late, sugar? You'll be exhausted tomorrow." Nana adjusted my wrap.

"Nana, I'll be fine."

"One more picture," Nana said. Austin put his arm around me and angled his head close. We said goodbye.

I picked up my overnight bag from the table in the foyer and walked outside. I could hear Nana say to Papa. "Our little girl's first dance."

On the way to the car, Austin laced his fingers through mine and whispered, "I can't wait for tonight."

I wanted to lose myself in the feeling of Austin's palm pressing against mine. It would be so much easier than thinking about all that had happened today, but I had to tell Austin about Micah's house.

Austin opened the door for me. We were driving to Hayden's to meet the limo. I hadn't invited my grandparents to take pictures there—too risky for them to be around the homecoming talk. I wished I didn't have to keep the parts of my life so separate, but maybe that was just what happened as people got older.

"I put the top up so the wind wouldn't mess your hair," Austin told me as he helped me into my seat.

"Thanks," I said. He grabbed my bag and stuck it on the backseat. I watched Austin walk around the car in the rearview mirror.

He turned on the car but didn't drive. Instead, he turned to me. "You look really good." He kissed me gently. So softly it wasn't enough. "Tonight is going to be amazing," he whispered.

He smelled like mint and rain and something else really good. I closed my eyes for a moment and pictured the end of the night. Austin sliding my wrap off my shoulders. Austin kissing the side of my neck. Snuggling next to him in bed. Sleeping in his arms.

He smiled slowly at me, in a way that made me think he knew what I was imagining. My face flushed. Then I shook my head. I shouldn't be thinking of that. Not when I still hadn't told him about Micah's house.

Austin pulled out of my driveway, and I took a deep breath. "The police were at Micah's this morning."

He let out a long exhale. "You heard?"

He knew?

I nodded.

"I was hoping you wouldn't find out so soon," he said. "I didn't want you to freak out."

He knew? "Austin, we have to tell," I said. "I mean, it's really serious. Do you know what Harrison did? And the police are involved. Maybe they'll go easier on us if we confess."

Austin shook his head. "I know it's bad, but think about it. It could wreck the rest of Harrison's life. And he told me he doesn't remember doing anything. I know he was drunk, but you'd remember that. So maybe it wasn't even him. Maybe someone else showed up later."

I wanted to believe that was possible, but the idea was ridiculous. Of course it had been Harrison.

"I'm not sure," I said.

"It was my fault in the first place, Essie." Austin rubbed his eye. I thought I heard a catch in his voice. "If the throw had been good . . . I can't ruin his life again."

I folded my hands in my lap, letting the soft fabric cradle them, letting Austin's words wash over me. Would this ruin Harrison's life? But what about Micah and Aunt Shelli and Uncle Steve?

"If they catch us, won't it be worse?" I asked.

"They won't catch us. None of us are ever going to talk about it again, to anyone. And if the police ask questions, which they won't, Hayden's parents think we were at her house the whole night. They'll say so. I know this sucks, Essie. But don't worry. It'll blow over soon."

I nodded, but my head felt dull and empty.

We parked on the street in front of Hayden's house, and before we got out of the car Austin kissed me softly on my forehead, then my nose, then my lips. "It'll be okay," he said. "I promise."

But I wasn't sure I knew what okay looked like anymore.

19

Before we started taking pictures, Hayden, Lara, and I went into the bathroom to freshen our makeup. Lara blotted her face with oil paper, and Hayden dabbed her lips with a gloss wand. "Austin told you what we talked about?" she asked me.

I nodded. "But I'm not sure if I can go through with it," I said.

Hayden turned around and put her hand on my shoulder. "This is the hardest part," she said. "I know it's scary and you feel like you are going to get caught, but if we all keep our mouths shut, we'll be fine."

"It's not the getting caught," I said, "so much as the guilt."

Hayden looked at me like I was a little kid. "Oh, please. If that's all it is, then you're fine. You barely threw any toilet paper. Give yourself a break."

I started to wonder if maybe she was right. It's not as if I meant for any of this to happen.

Lara looked my reflection up and down with a sneer on her face. "You are *not* going to say anything." She put her oil paper away and pulled out her mascara. "Anyway, it would be your word against the six of us. *And* Hayden's parents. We'll just say Austin dumped you, and you're trying to get back at him. No one will believe you."

"What?"

Lara shrugged and rolled her eyes at me. "I know you've got some secret thing going on with Micah. You think if you choose him over us Austin's really going to stand by you?"

My mouth hung open. I couldn't think of anything to say. I knew that was giving Lara the reaction she wanted, but I couldn't help myself. I felt dizzy.

"You have to choose, Essie," Lara said. "Micah or us."

Her words almost made me gag. I'd already chosen them over Micah, when I'd gone with Austin to Micah's house instead of making him stay in the van. But I'd made a mistake. Lara's words made it clear that I didn't matter to any of them. Maybe not even to Austin.

I looked at Hayden. She smiled and shrugged. "Sorry. It's nothing personal."

There was a knock at the door. "Girls, everyone's waiting," Hayden's mom called to us. "You're beautiful enough. Let's go."

Lara dropped her mascara in her purse, and Hayden wrapped her arms around both of us. "Group hug," she said. "This is going to be such an awesome night."

THE THEME OF THE DANCE was "Fall into Romance." The community house was decorated in burnt orange, burgundy, and gold, with candles everywhere. Our group was one of the last to arrive. Lara, Harrison, Hayden, and John had gotten completely drunk in the limo on the way to the restaurant and had been loud and obnoxious for the past hour and a half.

They drank even more in the limo on the way to the dance, and Hayden could barely stand in line to get her picture taken. John took her to sit down, while the rest of us waited our turn. After we posed in front of fake tree branches for our memento snapshot, the DJ put on "Get the Party Started," and Austin pulled me onto the dance floor. At first we were the only ones out there. I wanted to run and hide; it felt like everyone in the room was watching. And I wasn't in the mood to dance, but Austin wouldn't let go of my hands.

"Don't make us sit down with them," he whispered. *Them*. Did he really think of it that way? If I told him the truth, who Micah really was, would it be us and them, or would it be me and them?

Austin tugged my hand and smiled in that way that made me completely helpless. And the beat of the music was infectious. I turned off my brain and let the rhythm tell my body what to do. Soon I was dancing like we were alone in my room. We didn't leave the dance floor the entire night.

The last dance of the evening was a slow song. Austin held me tightly and rubbed his chin on my shoulder. His neck smelled like sweat and the scent made my insides pulse like the music we'd danced to earlier. After the song ended, I didn't want to lose that closeness. Austin must have felt the same way, because as he walked behind me to the coat check to get our things, he kept his arms around me. I didn't want to go to the hotel party anymore. I just wanted to dance with Austin for the rest of the night.

Austin squeezed my hand. "I can't wait to be alone with you," he whispered. His breath tickled the back of my neck. I couldn't wait either. I wished there wasn't a party. I didn't want to spend any time with them. I wanted it to be us, alone.

THE LIMO dropped everyone off at the hotel except for Austin and me. We went to Hayden's to get his car, and then drove back for the party. The parking lot was quiet and empty when we got there. I had expected to see someone hanging out in front the way they did at Hayden's, but you probably couldn't do that at a hotel. Sean's van was parked by the Dumpster.

Inside, the lobby was as deserted as the parking lot. The clerk at the front desk looked up at us as we walked in. Austin grabbed my arm and steered me toward a hallway with elevators.

"This way," he said. When we were out of sight of the clerk, he let go and pushed the up button. "Hayden's dad gave me the key. We're not supposed to be here without adults."

The hallway on the third floor was silent. No muffled music or laughter, no sign of any other people at all. My hands were fidgety, so I played with the zipper on my duffel while Austin slid the key card into the lock. Suddenly, I knew what the silence meant.

There was no party. I tried to think back to when he'd asked me to go to the hotel and realized he'd never said we'd be with other people. Sara's words echoed in my thoughts. *What do you think he expects?*

Austin walked into the room, but I didn't follow. He sat down on the edge of the double bed and looked at me standing in the doorway.

"Come here," he said. "I have something for you." He rummaged through his duffel and produced a turquoise box tied with a white ribbon.

I forced my feet one at a time into the room and shut the door behind me. It was heavy and closed with a thud that reminded me of a bank vault being sealed shut. Moments ago, I'd been dreading the party, but now that I knew it wasn't happening, I was worried. I walked over to Austin. I couldn't wait to see what he'd give me, but part of me didn't really want to know.

"I wanted to show you how special tonight is to me." He handed me the gift, and with one tug, the silky ribbon slipped from the package down to the floor. The box contained a silver heart on a chain. ESSIE was engraved on one side and AUSTIN engraved on the other.

Everything inside of me trembled. "Thank you. It's beautiful."

"Let me help you put it on." Austin took the necklace from me and fastened it at the back of my neck. He kissed me softly on the nape when he was finished. It made me lose my breath. I wanted to kiss him so much, but once I did, would I be able to stop? Tonight there was no curfew, no lights flicking on from the porch, no driving lessons.

My breath grew shallow.

"Want to watch *Saturday Night Live*?" he asked, grabbing the remote from the night table and turning on the TV.

I could have cried from relief. "Yes." A lump filled my throat, but I swallowed it down, and kept nodding. "I just want to hang up my dress before it gets ruined."

I went to the bathroom to change into an oversized T-shirt and flannel pajama bottoms, while Austin waited for me on the bed. I decided to leave my bra on. I could hear him laughing at the TV as I washed the makeup off my face. I felt stupid for reacting the way I did before. Austin didn't expect anything. He knew how I felt. We were going to watch TV. Just because we were staying in the same room didn't mean we were going to go all the way.

I stepped out of the bathroom. Austin had changed, too. Now he wore gray sweatpants and his senior class T-shirt. He sat propped up against the headboard.

"Hey," he said.

My knees nearly gave way. "Hey," I answered. I turned around to put my duffel in the closet and hide how flustered I felt.

"You want some beer? I've got a six-pack in the minifridge."

I shook my head. I was already lying to my grandparents and spending the night in a hotel room with my boyfriend. That was enough bad behavior.

"Come watch with me," he said.

I walked over to the bed, wobbly, like I was still wearing heels, and snuggled next to him. We watched the rest of the show nestled together like spoons.

We were on the same bed. Together. In our pajamas.

The show ended, and Austin turned off the TV. He scooted forward and laid his head on the pillow. I lay down next to him, the bedspread scratchy through my shirt. Austin turned over onto his side. I could feel him looking at me, but I kept my eyes on a scuff mark on the ceiling. How does a scuff mark even get onto a ceiling?

"Essie." Austin said my name so softly it was like a blanket surrounding us, warm and safe. Maybe the whole night would be warm and safe, too.

He kissed me. I let the soft feeling wash over me as we kissed some more. His hands went to my chest. I took a deep breath in and let the shell of worry that had been encasing my body, keeping me from feeling too much, crack open. Suddenly, all I could do was feel; my insides went warm and fluid as lava. Austin grabbed the bottom of my shirt and slid it up over my head. He took his shirt off, too, and pressed his skin against mine.

And then, my body tensed. My thoughts suddenly caught up with my emotions.

Were we going to go all the way? My body wanted to, but my brain was sending out error messages all over the place.

You need protection.

It's going to hurt!

Once you do it, you can never go back.

You'll be a grown-up.

It was the last one that threw me. I closed my eyes and turned my head away.

Austin slid his hand down to my hip, hooking his thumb into the top of my pajama pants. The delicious softness from before was gone.

"I'll be right back," Austin said, his voice husky in his throat. My breath caught. It felt so good when he kissed me, but so scary when he wanted more.

I hugged the pillow tightly and listened to Austin go into the bathroom and close the door. Then I heard a shuffling sound and Austin clearing his throat. What was he doing? Getting a condom?

My mind raced. Everything I'd ever heard about him and heard him say to me was circling my brain.

He's a player.

He's always into somebody.

You're not like other girls.

The biggest male slut in the school.

You're the first girl who's wanted to wait.

He dumped Vi when she wouldn't sleep with him.

His friends shunned her.

If we wait, it'll be more special.

Austin returned. I kept my eyes shut.

"Essie?" he whispered.

A deep sigh escaped my lips. I didn't know how to answer. I couldn't find the words I needed to say. So I didn't open my eyes, and I didn't say anything, just listened to the sound of my pulse throbbing.

Austin rubbed my leg. "Are you asleep?"

I opened my eyes. "I'm awake," I whispered. "I just don't think I can do this."

Austin kneeled by the side of the bed and touched my cheek. "I won't let anything happen to you."

"No, Austin, I can't." I sat up and shook my head. My ears felt hot and red, like all my shame was focused there.

He put his hand on my neck and a tingle ran up my scalp. His face was so close to mine I thought he was going to kiss me, but he whispered, "Don't you want to be back where we were five minutes ago?"

His mouth was less than an inch from mine, his breath soft and even on my lips. I wanted to inhale it, inhale him. But I didn't trust myself. Or Austin. Not completely.

"I want to," I said. "But . . ." I shook my head.

Austin sighed and laid his forehead on the edge of the bed. "Okay," he said.

"I'm sorry." I rested my fingertips on his shoulder. My heart felt thin. I traced my index finger over his back. I-M S-O-R-R-Y.

"Essie?" Austin sat up and looked straight into my eyes. "I love you," he whispered.

My eyes welled up, and I pressed my lips hard against his. He groaned and climbed onto the bed, and in the heat of the kisses I realized what it was I'd just done.

Sara flashed through my mind. I wished I had listened to her, believed her. I wished she knew what I was about to do. I felt like I was taking a trip, and no one knew where I was going. It was unsettling, and gave me the feeling that I was about to disappear off the face of the earth.

Or maybe I was becoming someone new. Someone I couldn't picture. And even though I knew it was silly, I was scared for a minute that no one would recognize me in the morning.

I pressed my skin against Austin's as hard as I could, to see if I could find that connected feeling again. Austin sighed and kissed my neck. I could feel him wanting me. And I wanted him too, sort of.

This was going to be my first time; it seemed crazy that I couldn't find that feeling. Wasn't that the whole point? So that I'd feel closer to Austin? The more I thought about it, the further away I felt. Until I was detached. Outside myself. Observing instead of feeling. My body and Austin were in their own little world, without *me*.

Austin slid his hands down my body. Would he be able to tell that I wasn't really there? *He should be able to tell,* a voice whispered at the back of my brain, *if he loves you.*

Silent tears slid from my eyes. Austin brushed his cheek against mine and the wetness smeared across both of our faces. He pulled back and stared at me. My body didn't feel sad; it felt empty. Austin held my gaze; I knew he would see it.

"I know," he whispered, stroking the hair next to my forehead. "It feels special to me, too." He brushed his lips against mine. "You are the first girl I've ever been in love with." He kissed both my tear-soaked cheeks, then slid his hand along my hip and over my underpants.

Suddenly I was back in my body. The saltwater from my tears had turned into an icy ocean inside me. I heard a voice clearly in my head. *Are you really going to have sex with him?* My body shivered. The question sounded like something Sara would ask, but it wasn't her voice. It was mine.

Stop! I thought.

It was like a dream. My thoughts were screaming, but my voice was paralyzed.

Stop!

Austin kissed my neck and my shoulder; his hand slipped between my knees.

Stop!

I pressed my legs together. Austin wiggled his fingers, teasing my thighs apart. The more he wiggled, the harder I squeezed. Suddenly I realized I was already in that other world, that world of being grown-up, and nobody was going to take care of me, or make decisions for me, but me.

"Wait!"

Austin's eyes sagged, like a puppy I'd just yelled at.

"Did I do something wrong?" he asked.

"No," I said. "Not wrong, but I really can't do this."

Austin sat up and moved to the other side of the bed. "We don't have to," he said.

"I don't just mean tonight. And I guess I don't just mean sex. I mean everything. Austin, I don't think I belong with you. I'm not like Hayden and Lara; they're not even my friends. I don't like to drink. And I'm not ready to have sex. It's too much pressure being the only girl who's ever asked you to wait. I'm not ready to handle that."

Austin's expression was shock and then sadness. He looked down at the bedspread.

"I'm just not like you guys. And I don't think I can keep Micah's house a secret either. It's wrong."

He looked up at me. His eyes were shiny.

"And . . . he's my cousin."

Austin's eyes went wide. "What?" He covered his face with his hands and shook his head. Finally he looked at me again. "Why didn't you tell me?"

"I didn't think you'd like me if you knew. He's so different. He doesn't belong in your group; I figured you'd think I was the same way."

"But that's what I liked about you in the first place. I'm sick of my friends. Sick of them always expecting me to be something I'm not."

The bed was miles long between us. I wanted to touch him,

but couldn't bring myself to do it. The necklace he gave me lay cold against my collarbone. I touched the silver heart. "Should I give this back to you?"

"Do you want to?"

"I don't, but I can't be the kind of girl you want to date. I don't know when I'll be ready to have sex and I know that's important to you."

"Essie, were you listening to anything I said? I'm not what you think I am." He looked up at the ceiling. "I'm a virgin, too."

I tried to process his words, but couldn't do anything more than blink in response.

"My brother is a player, and everyone assumes I'm the same. Every girl I date is ready to sleep with me practically the first time we go out. It's a turnoff. When I visit my brother at college, I see him sleep with girls too drunk to even know what's happening. I don't want it to be like that for me."

"But you've dated a million girls," I said. "The whole school knows that you've slept with them. Except Vi. You broke up with her because she wouldn't sleep with you."

"It's not true. Vi broke up with me. She hated my friends, and I was too chicken to choose her over them."

It was just like Lara said. *You think he'll choose you over us?*

"I have to tell my aunt the truth about her house," I said, holding my breath. What would he say? That I was on my own? Six against one?

He nodded. "I guess I do, too. I can't make excuses for Harrison anymore."

20

The next morning Austin dropped me off down the block from my house. We'd agreed that I'd tell Aunt Shelli and then Austin would tell Harrison what we planned to do, to give him a chance to turn himself in to the police. I didn't think he'd take it, but Austin said he didn't have a choice. I kissed Austin goodbye and told him I didn't know when I'd be able to talk again. I had no idea what would happen after I confessed.

As I came through my front door, shaking with nerves, the phone started ringing.

"I'm home," I called.

I heard Nana in the kitchen answering the phone.

"Sara, hi," she said. "Yes, she just came in. I didn't even hear your car!" Nana walked into the foyer, where I stood with one foot on the bottom stair. She handed me the phone. "Where is she calling from? The driveway?"

I shrugged and took the receiver. That was close. What if Sara had called five minutes earlier? And why wasn't she calling my cell phone?

"Hi," I said, going up the stairs.

"Hi," Sara said. Her voice sounded sharp.

"Hi," I said again.

There was a pause. "Is there something you want to tell me?"

Actually, her voice sounded mad. I didn't say anything.

"Well, then," Sara continued, "let me tell you about my night. I went over to Micah's house after dinner to work on our chemistry homework. Guess who was there? Your grandparents. And guess what they said to me as soon as they saw me?"

Sara went to Micah's? How on earth was I supposed to know that Sara would be going over to Micah's?

"The second I walked in the door, they said, 'Isn't Essie going to be at your house soon?' "

"What'd you say?" I poked my head out of my door. I could hear Nana in the kitchen doing dishes. Aunt Shelli had probably already known Sara was coming over. That's why she'd been giving me those funny looks.

"I shouldn't have," Sara said. "But I covered for you. You know all about covering for people, right? I had to turn around and go home an hour later so that I could 'hang out' with you. Thanks."

I sat down on my bedroom floor. Every limb in my body weighed a thousand pounds. On top of everything, I'd been a bad friend to Sara more times than I could count. I doubted it would do any good, but I finally owed her the truth.

"I was at Micah's house the night it was toilet-papered."

"O-kay . . ." she answered, as though she was waiting for me to say more.

00.

"Harrison is the one who trashed the house. I'm going to tell my aunt today."

I didn't hear anything but silence coming from Sara's end of the phone. Had our call been dropped? "Sara?"

"I'm here," she said.

"I'm really sorry. I completely screwed up, but I miss you. There's so much I want to tell you." There was so much I still needed to be forgiven for. It would take a long time to regain her trust, but I had to try. "Will you meet me for coffee later?"

It seemed like hours before Sara finally gave her answer.

"Should I pick you up at one?"

Relief washed over me; I wanted to hug my phone. "I'll be ready."

A SHORT WHILE LATER Nana knocked on my door.

I opened it so quickly she jumped back a bit.

"Oh, Essie! Are you off the phone? That was fast. What did Sara need to talk about anyway, one second after dropping you off?"

I thought about telling Nana everything right then. I was about to confess to Aunt Shelli, but telling Nana was different. And besides, Nana was still keeping a secret from me.

"Uh, I left something in her car. It's no big deal. She's going to bring it by later."

I looked down at my feet. Maybe it was time to start showing her the truth. Let her see what was really happening to me.

"Look what Austin gave me," I said. I put my hand underneath the silver heart, and Nana peered at it closely.

"It says *Austin*," she said. "He gave you a necklace with his name on it?"

That was all she could see. I moved my hand so that the pendant was hidden inside my fist. The distance between the way I really was and the way Nana saw me kept growing bigger and bigger.

Nana reached out and ran her fingers through my hair, nails tickling my scalp, like she was remembering when I was younger and I used to ask her to scratch my head. "You'll always be my little girl," she said.

Maybe it was just impossible for Nana to realize that I was changing. Seeing her pale blue eyes filled with love, I wished I could stay the same for her, but I knew I couldn't.

"I love you, Nana," I said, burying my head in her shoulder.

Nana tickled her fingernails over my back and kissed my forehead. "Mmmm, you're still delicious," she said. "Just like when you were a baby."

I hugged her tighter and she squeezed me back, then let go.

"I'm going to the grocery store. Do you want to come?" she asked.

"I need to go to Micah's," I said.

Nana smiled. "What a nice idea. I'll come, too."

"No." It came out louder than I meant it to, and Nana's face fell, but I didn't change my mind. "I need to go by myself. I have something important I need to tell them, and then when I come home, I'll tell you."

"What is it?" Nana's eyes looked panicky, and I wanted to reassure her, but there wasn't that much I could say.

"Nana, I have to tell them first."

Her eyes misted. "I'll be in my room when you get home," she said. "Papa can drive you."

I might have felt guiltier, except that I knew what I'd tell her later would be a lot worse, and I was too scared about what was going to happen when I got to my aunt and uncle's house.

I ASKED PAPA if he wouldn't mind just dropping me off. I walked up to their front porch alone and Micah opened the door.

"What are you doing here?" he asked, clearly not happy to see me.

"I need to talk to your mom," I said. "And to you."

Micah folded his arms across his chest, but didn't move out of the doorway to let me inside. Papa was just pulling away from the house. I wondered if he noticed.

"Did you have a good time last night?" Micah asked, his voice full of sarcasm. "My plans were cut short. Oh yeah, that was your fault, too."

"I told Austin that you're my cousin last night," I said. "And that I had to tell the truth about what happened to your house."

Micah squinted his eyes at me, still distrustful. "Why?" he asked.

"Because it's true," I said. "You are my cousin. And because it was the right thing to do. And because maybe you'll never be my brother, but I don't want you to hate me. I want us to at least be friends."

Micah leaned against the doorframe. "I don't know if I can forgive you."

I took a deep breath. "I know," I said.

Micah nodded. His eyebrows relaxed. "Okay, then." He stepped aside and motioned me into the house. I followed him into the family room, where Aunt Shelli and Uncle Steve were watching the Sunday morning news shows.

Aunt Shelli muted the television. "Essie! What are you doing here?"

Uncle Steve stood up and switched off the TV. "Did something happen?" he asked.

I shook my head. "I need to talk to Aunt Shelli."

My aunt shot a worried look at my uncle, but she said, "Sure. Why don't we go up to my room so we can have some privacy."

I followed Aunt Shelli upstairs and sat down on the bed next to her. My voice quivered as I spoke. "I was at your house Friday night."

I watched Aunt Shelli's face, to see if she hated me, but other than pressing her lips together, her expression didn't change. She didn't say anything either, so I kept talking.

"I thought we were just going to throw toilet paper. I didn't want to, but I let myself be talked into it, which I know I shouldn't have done. I didn't know about the other stuff until yesterday. But I know that's not really an excuse." I shook my head. "I'll pay you back, and I'll tell the police everything. I'm really sorry."

I looked down at my knees then, because if Aunt Shelli couldn't forgive me, I didn't want to know it. Two months ago I thought I didn't care if she was in my life, but now the idea of not having her felt like a punishment.

I heard Aunt Shelli take a long, slow breath. "I'll forgive you, if you can forgive me."

I blinked back tears. "Forgive you for what?"

"After your grandparents got custody of you, I shouldn't have let myself be caught up in hurt feelings and resentment. We shouldn't have moved away. We should have been here for you."

"But I don't understand. What happened?"

"When your parents died, they didn't have a will. It was so hard for me to conceive Micah, and I'd been trying to have another child unsuccessfully. Steve and I thought it made perfect sense that you should live with us. But your grandparents wanted you to live with them. Nana had been watching you two days a week already, while your parents worked, so they argued that it would be less confusing for you."

Aunt Shelli took my hand and pressed it to her lips before continuing. "Our lawyer argued that your grandparents were too old, and that your parents would have wanted you to have a Jewish upbringing, but Nana and Papa had stopped going to synagogue and had no plans to return. Their lawyer said that your parents wouldn't have wanted you to be raised in the strictly observant home Steve and I had then created. Steve had taken off a year of work to study Torah. At that time he was thinking about going to rabbinical school or moving to Israel."

Aunt Shelli paused and squeezed my hand again. "Are you sure you want to hear all this?"

Every muscle in my body was so rigid it hurt, and each breath I took sent shockwaves through my chest, but I nodded at her. I had to know.

"Well, after that, things just got crazy. Each side dug up every nasty thing it could about the other. Very, very hurtful things were said, and in the end, the judge decided you should live with Nana and Papa. Uncle Steve decided he couldn't go back to work with his father, and we moved to New York."

A tear ran down my aunt's cheek. "We all lost sight of what was truly important," Aunt Shelli said. "You." Then she stood up, went to her dresser, and pulled a small jewelry box out of the bottom drawer.

"I bought this for you for Hanukkah," she said. "But I'd like to give it to you now."

The box wasn't wrapped, so I lifted the lid. Inside was a golden Hebrew word on a chain.

"It says *Esther*," she said, then looked at my neck. "Oh! You already have a special necklace."

"It's new," I said. "My boyfriend gave it to me last night."

Aunt Shelli picked it up and looked at both sides. "It's beautiful," she said. "I didn't realize your relationship was that serious. Would you like me to exchange mine for something else?"

I shook my head. For the first time in my life, I felt like I was starting to understand, in a small way, who I was. I was the girl my grandmother saw, and the girl on the heart necklace with Austin. I was the girl who'd gotten lost in a family feud and who'd been found again. And somewhere, deep inside, I was Esther. "I'd like to wear both," I told my aunt. "Will you help me put it on?"

Aunt Shelli draped the necklace around my neck. It fell comfortably just below the other one.

"When I was little," I told Aunt Shelli, "after you moved, I used to pretend you were coming back to get me." I looked at my feet, embarrassed.

"I did come back." Aunt Shelli squeezed my shoulder. "It just took a long time."

PAPA CAME TO pick me up about an hour later. I didn't know if I should tell him or Nana that I knew about the custody case. Would it change anything between us if I told? As we drove home, I fingered my new necklace and a question popped into my mind.

"How come you decided not to take me to synagogue or teach me about being Jewish?" I pressed my forehead against the window and watched the houses roll by.

"I was angry after your parents died. Angry for a long time. I hated that Judaism didn't have any answers for me. No religion could make my pain go away or bring your parents back. I hated our religion, and I blamed it for your parents' death."

"But why didn't Nana take me?"

"It was too hard for her to go back to our synagogue, where your parents used to belong. And I wasn't willing to start at a new one."

"Oh." I guessed that made sense, but it was so different from what I'd imagined. I always thought I'd been raised the way I was because they thought it was better for me. Really it was just better for them. I breathed hard on the window until I'd created a big foggy patch, then with the tip of my finger traced a question mark into the glass. I didn't know what to do now. I didn't want to become as Jewish as Uncle Steve, but it seemed like Sara was right. At least I should learn something about who I was.

WHEN WE GOT HOME, Nana was waiting at the foot of the stairs in her bathrobe. "Are you going to tell me what's going on?" she said.

I took a deep breath. "I had to go to Aunt Shelli's to tell her that I was at her house on Friday night when it got trashed."

Nana flinched. I could see myself transforming in her eyes, from tap-dancing granddaughter to the kind of teenager on trashy talk shows who needed to be sent to boot camp because she couldn't be controlled. Neither of which was really me.

Nana opened her mouth, but no words came out. She looked at Papa, something desperate in her eyes.

"Nana, I made a mistake, but I'm trying to fix it. Isn't that part of growing up? I'm not a kid anymore."

"You're only fifteen."

"I'll be sixteen soon."

Nana shook her head. "I have to go lie down again," she said. She turned and went upstairs. She wouldn't ever see me the same way she used to, but as hard as it was, it was also a good thing. I wasn't that four-year-old who needed a judge to decide what was best for her. It was time for me to decide.

I turned to Papa. "I'm going to need you to sign a form," I said. "I want to take driver's ed."

21

Six months later, after completing driver's ed and logging fifty hours of supervised driving time, mostly with Aunt Shelli, I was ready to get my license. A month after my sixteenth birthday. On a Friday afternoon, Aunt Shelli picked me up early from school and we went for lunch. Then I drove her red minivan to the secretary of state's office and took my exam. The smile in my picture when I was finished was so big I looked like my face was half teeth, but I didn't care.

When I drove Aunt Shelli's car back to my house, I couldn't believe what I saw on the driveway. Nana's navy Honda Accord with a big bow on top.

"Calm down, calm down," Nana said when I ran inside screaming. "And don't thank me. This was all Papa's idea."

"Now that I'm retired, we don't need both cars," he said, kissing me and handing me the keys.

"I bought you a new dress," Nana said. "Want to go try it on?"

"I can't, Nana." My hands were itching to grab the steering

wheel. "I'll be back for the party, okay?" I hadn't wanted to celebrate my birthday until I got my license.

Nana pouted, but Papa kissed my cheek, and I was off. I climbed into the front seat and adjusted it. I fiddled with the rearview mirror and started the car. Before I backed out of the driveway, I changed all the radio presets. Then I turned the volume way up, and I drove. I wasn't going anywhere in particular. I wanted to be in the car by myself, moving, feeling the road slip back underneath me. I turned down nearly every street in Pershing until it was almost four o'clock. My birthday party was going to be early, at four-thirty. Afterward we'd light candles for Shabbat.

I had one more stop before heading home. I pulled in front of Austin's house and honked my horn. He poked his head out of the front door and opened his eyes wide in shock.

"Nice ride," he said as he walked toward the car.

I rolled down the passenger window. "Want a lift?" I asked.

Austin nodded and walked all the way around my car, inspecting it. Then he kicked the rear tires and gave me the thumbs-up.

"Get in," I called. "I can't be late for my own party."

Austin climbed in next to me and glanced around the car's interior.

"Roomy backseat," he said with a smile.

"Feel free to sit back there by yourself," I answered, easing out of the driveway. "I'll be staying behind the wheel."

MY SIXTEENTH BIRTHDAY PARTY was pretty small. There were only nine people in the world that I wanted with me, so that's who I invited. Aunt Shelli and Uncle Steve. Micah and Sara. Nana and Papa. Zoe, Skye, and, of course, Austin.

I set up my iPod and speakers in the family room, and we let the music seep into our skin and get us moving. Aunt Shelli was a great dancer. Uncle Steve moved a little like a robot, but he was trying. That counted for something.

Sara and Micah were lost in their own world, slow dancing even when the beat was thumping. They'd been dating a few months now. Aunt Shelli loved Sara. Uncle Steve was still getting used to the idea.

Papa carried out my cake while everyone sang "Happy Birthday" to me. I closed my eyes and blew out the candles, but I didn't make a wish. I had everything I wanted. I opened my eyes and took it all in.

ACKNOWLEDGMENTS

Thanks to Brenda Ferber, Carol Coven Grannick, and Ellen Reagan, who read and commented on this book more times than any three people should ever have to read an unfinished book. To Rabbi Karyn Kedar for our weekly Book of Esther sessions. To Coach Steve Winiecki for explaining the workings of a high school football team and for letting me spy on his football practice. To Coach Jenny Navickas for teaching a non-cheerleader to appreciate cheerleading. And to attorney Michael Goldberg for guiding me through the ins and outs of grandparent custody.

Thanks to my friends and family, who gave me fantastic insights, suggestions, and plain old love and support: Amy and Jenna Bazelon, Stephen Yafa, Judy Tigay, Helen Meyerhoff, Sarah Hirsch, Donnie Stutland, Barry Tigay, Dave Tigay, Shari Helmer, Rebecca Handel-Fano, Kelly Goldberg, Anjali Polan, Joe Tigay, Ben Tigay, Julie Tigay, Jill Meyerhoff, Jim Meyerhoff, Emma Meyerhoff, Adam Meyerhoff, and Noah Meyerhoff.

And finally, thanks to the three different editors who put me through a marathon of revision: Beverly Reingold, Jill Davis, and Janine O'Malley. I'm grateful that I got to work with each of you and with everyone at FSG. An author couldn't ask for more.

You are all truly appreciated.